I0622261

BELLA DONNA

OPHELIA FINSEN

Also by Ophelia Finsen:

Lovers of Old Films
This is Living
Society of Lost Causes
The Women of Jimanac
Skye
The Romanian
At the Upper Villa Tyde
Perception
You Stole My Thunder

2

Once upon a time, many years ago there was a man, and there was a woman. From the first moment they saw one another they were consumed by a great burning passion. To be apart was torture. They needed to be together with nothing, not even clothing between them. This was many years ago, before many terrible events and in those days men and women couldn't live together until they were married. It was simply not the thing to do.

The bans were read in the church as soon as it was possible. The set wedding date crept towards them excruciatingly slowly. But married they were, and that honeymoon, that month of honey, was a time of intense passion, on endless repeat. Had any man loved any woman quite as much? Had any woman loved a man to such an extent?

If this were a fairy story, they could have continued thus for an eternity. But this is an account of real life, and they had to return to the community and the everyday routine. It looked like a good prospect. Now he was married, the man's status at work improved. His wage increased and he was given a cottage to live in. They moved to the forest where he worked. The woman was happy with her new home and allowance from her husband. Here she lived with her man and his colleagues, in the forest gang village. In the day time she had the company of the other wives and the children. At night she had her man. They were so deep in the wide stretching forest that they could forget the rest of the world existed.

During the following months of wedded bliss they had the time to get to know one another. A passionate lover he might have been, but he was not one for great conversation. She began to wonder how much she liked this simple minded woodsman. He grew tired of her moaning, her complaints and demands, and watched as his wife's neat waist broadened and slackened, and her stomach began to expand. Their passion weakened and was replaced with regret. They had wanted each other, but now they only wanted themselves. He remembered an old saying he had heard people laughing about. Marry in haste, repent at leisure. So this is what they had meant.

The comments and sniping evolved into arguments and screaming. They couldn't bear to be in the same house, but they had nowhere to go. There was no way to escape one another. Whenever there was a domestic problem in the village the same action was always taken. Like small children workers and wives ran shouting and crying to the gang supervisor. He had to solve this. He had to make her stop screaming. He had to explain what the Jones' ought to do with their children. How much was enough to spend at Christmas? Her husband had drunk away the money and they still had days before he was paid again and no food in the cupboard. What were the children to eat? The previous gang supervisor had been an old man who had done the job for decades. He had taken it all in his stride. The new gang supervisor was straight out of college, as yet an unmarried man, and overwhelmed by all of the questions. He had studied forest management. He didn't know a thing about wailing babies, marriage counselling and at what point it was a drink too far.

When the man told the supervisor he could not stand to be with his wife anymore, he did not know what to say. When the wife arrived saying she hated her demanding baby and wanted to go away back to the city, he told her things would get easier. He had no idea.

It was early in the morning, whilst the mist still twisted around the trees and crept out into the forest village. Whilst workers, even the early risers still slept, and the birds blinked and contemplated the dawn chorus. Whilst the sun had yet to warm the earth. The woman crept up to the gang supervisor's cottage with a bundle of sobbing rags. The babe was only days old but it had an instinctive awareness that it was not wanted. The knowledge broke its heart. The woman laid the bundle on the doorstep. There was a note on the kitchen table for her sleeping husband. Go fetch your child and care for it. I have left and I do not intend to return. With suitcase in her hand, she left the village without a backward glance.

What she did not realise is that the humped masses of her sleeping husband – for they had stopped sharing a bed months ago – was nothing more than a bundle of sheets and blankets with thumped pillows bulking out the form. The man had left in twilight. The babe's crying was too much to stand. He regretted his marriage. His head hung low at the mocking jeering of his fellow woodsmen. He had to get away from everything and start again, but he was not sure if it would be allowed. Fleeing at night seemed like his only option. He went for the coast and took to the seas and ended his days in Patagonia.

When the gang supervisor woke to bright sunshine, he felt as though a weight had been lifted. He did not know why. He strode out onto his clear doorstep and looked around the peaceful village. The young couple were not screaming this morning. Perhaps they had made their peace. As they were to discover later in the day, the young family had actually fled, and with a week's wages owing too. All in the village assumed they had left as a collective. The man and the woman never wondered what had happened to the babe on the doorstep.

Her hair was tatty, for she had neglected to brush it before leaving her cottage. She had not been sleeping well of late. With the first dawning drabs of light she considered leaving her bed. She decided to begin her foraging early that day. With bag and basket, herself wrapped up in shawls, she left her home and strode out in the depths of the wild woodland. This was a realm beyond the areas controlled by the foresters and outside the remit of the stately home grounds to the north. She came from the forgotten borders.

She walked fast, picking at mushrooms and berries, herbs and roots as she went, feeling the satisfaction of a fruitful forage. She moved further than usual, coming upon an area recently cleared by felling. She was still too early for the woodsmen. Sitting upon an ample tree stump, she took out a small clay pipe and enjoyed a quiet ten minutes listening to the forest and watching the grey smoke twist up from her pipe. Knocking the remnants out by tapping the pipe against the side of the stump, she packed away her belongings and continued on the trek.

The recent felling and loss of trees altered her understanding of the land, and she caught her breath as she came out of the woodland and into the forest village. She had not meant to wander so far. She did not care for the company of people, and although she would go to the town out of necessity now and then, she preferred to arrive mysteriously, so that no one would quite be able to work out where she lived. She avoided the woodsmen the most; for they were the ones most likely to discover her should they know she was out there in the depths of the ancient woodland.

Up the track, five miles to the nearest regular village (rather than the purpose built forestry village) she noted a retreating figure carrying a suitcase. The life of the forest did not suit all. She smiled wryly to herself. This was a secret departure, for the rest of the woodsmen and their wives had not yet risen. She moved to turn away, but a cry stopped her. It had come from outside, not contained within the buildings. Soundlessly she crept down the side of a building and around to the front of the gang supervisor's house, wondering what had made the noise. She stumbled on her own surprise as she saw the newborn, bundled in sparse rags, discarded on a doorstep. She leant forward and peered down into the bundle. The child, suddenly quiet by this new arrival, gazed up at the stranger. The woman's expression softened. Here was a beautiful child, perhaps the most beautiful ever born. Who could dispose of such a creature like this?

The baby started to fuss. "Now, now," the woman said gently. Shrugging off one of her shawls, she wrapped the baby up and lifted it so they could consider one another eye to eye in the proper manner. A baby left on the doorstep would find itself in an orphanage, or with the nuns. Perhaps it would be taken in with one of the other woodland families, a second class citizen to the proper children. To be abused and taken advantage of. She stroked the child's soft cheek. She had always wanted a child of her own, but circumstance had dictated it was not to be.

"*Demat,*" she said to the child. "*Ahes eo ma anv.*"

The child looked blank.

"You do not understand?" She asked in accented English. "No worry. You will learn. I said good morning, and that my name is Ahes."

This appeared to mean more to the child.

"And I believe you are Isobella."

Ahes held Isobella close to her, and hurried away from the forest village. And with that, both their destinies were decided.

Once upon a time there was a beautiful woman called Ahes Omnes. She was born on the coast in the north-west of France. It was a time when the old ways were starting to die out, but her grandmother made certain that Ahes learned the old skills and the true language of their people. When Ahes started the village school her French was a little shaky but she was a bright child and soon spoke the national language like a native. But in her heart she was always Breton.

And so she grew up to the sound of the sea, wandering along the cliffs and the shoreline. She was curious as to what lay beyond the sea, beyond the horizon. But never curious enough to dare to set sail alone. And perhaps she would have always stayed there, married a fisherman and produced a line of scruffy children, had it not been for the Irish.

Years later, she couldn't remember why they had come, their distant Celtic cousins. They spoke a beautiful language that sounded familiar but incomprehensible. Breton and Irish had separated too long ago and the break had been too deep to allow for any mutual understanding to remain. The Irish boy spoke French to her. He had beautiful eyes, long lashes, and a broad smile that made her forget what she had been thinking of a moment ago. The young Ahes had never known love before, and ignorant to the pains it can cause, she let herself fall bodily and spiritually into the pool of infatuation. They walked hand in hand by the sea. He told her of the green fields of Ireland, the windswept coast, the music, the magic. She could not think of anything else when they were parted. She could neither eat nor sleep. He was more important to her well being than the air in her lungs and the blood in her veins.

He would soon be leaving for *Angleterre*, and the Emerald Isle beyond. They agreed they must be married, for she could not leave with him any other way. Her family were suspicious and concerned. Ahes was still young and too consumed with first love. She did not think rationally. She did not want to be rational. She said she had found her purpose in life. The two were married; Ahes Omnes and her Patrick Donagh became one. Grinning like fools, they left Ahes' homeland and set sail for foreign lands.

They travelled through southern England and Wales, and took the ship across to Ireland. They went back to the small stone village where he hailed from, and in a storm of cheers and music and dance, she was accepted into the Donagh family. It was a beautiful place, but one cannot live on fresh air and fine views alone and they had to move to one of the east coast towns for work. Here some people spoke the beautiful language of the Irish, but the predominant tongue was English. Breton meant nothing to the inhabitants, and French little. Ahes learnt English. Patrick worked. She kept house. They waited for the children, but the years ticked by and nothing came. Ahes continued to bleed with the alarming regularity of a chaste virgin. They did not know what the problem was and did not dare speak of it together in fear that raising the subject would open disappointment and they would part. Patrick spent more time in the pubs to avoid the melancholia of his wife. Ahes took to wandering by the sea in solitude. Their silence absorbed them.

Only one or two knew the location of Ahes forest cottage, and of those who knew, only Ahes cared or gave a thought to the little building. It was so deep within the sprawling forest as to be forgotten to time. It was beyond the reach of the forest gang's working remit, and so far from the boundaries of the rich estates, that it resided in a no man's land. So far from what the local landowners could see from their country palaces, that most had forgotten this patch of land even existed.

In ancient woodland, down a bank and hidden by the curve of the land and the twist of gnarled trees, the stone cottage had stood for centuries. It had been abandoned for countless years, and when Ahes had found it, half the roof was gone and the windows were dead dark holes. Nettles grew in the doorway.

She was a practical woman, raised to look after herself and solve her own problems. She had money at that point. She'd bought what she'd needed at the nearest town and secretively taken her goods into the forest. She made sure no one saw the path she took. Over the summer she restored the cottage, fixing the walls and the roof, installing a level wooden floor, windows and clearing the chimney and fireplace in readiness for meals and the coming winter. She built a lean-to woodshed and dug the garden clear of weeds and forest refuse. Most of the planting would start the next year, for now she could only plant some winter crops and rely on her supplies from the town. She cleared out some of the canopy to be sure of a good supply of sunlight on her garden. It was a secret forest glade. With the timber she felled, she constructed rudimentary furniture for her home. Ahes had reached a point in her life where she had no need of people and the civilised world.

By the time Isobella came to live with her, Ahes was well established with seven years in residence. During her first winter a black cat with white paws had appeared by the wood store one day, and had since taken up residence in the house. She would disappear into the forest most days, taking care of her own diet, but returning to sleep by the fire on a winter's evening, or on a summer's night to gambol in the garden whilst Ahes lay back by the camomile and enjoyed the sound of birdsong.

Isobella was a noisy addition to their small collective. It worried the cat for the first few weeks before they fell into an understanding. Isobella grew from a noisy baby to a curious toddler and a quiet and thoughtful child. She saw no one but Ahes, who was teacher and mother. They spoke Breton in this land far from Ahes' home, but as Ahes would say, *Ur yezh hepken n'eo ket a-walc'h*, and she made certain Isobella understood English and French just as well. One language is never enough.

Ahes grew a wide variety of herbs, fruits and vegetables in her garden and knew how to forage from the forest. She could cure a great many ails and sicknesses, and passed down her understanding of plant lore to her daughter. Both mother and daughter were dark haired and thoughtful, and Isobella was never to know that in truth she had a different parentage.

In summer days Isobella would run through the garden, dashing through bursts of butterflies, chasing the cat and eating peas fresh from the pods. She was curious about everything that grew, fingers dabbling in the earth, pulling at leaves and roots to sample their scents and tastes. Only a long narrow bed in the shade of the trees at a corner of the cottage was not for play. Here tall, woody plants grew, with long green leaves and small purple flowers almost lost to the size of the leaves. Green berries would appear on the plants, ripening to a tempting shiny black. Ahes told her this plant deserved respect, and that it was the owner of the cottage. When she had first cleared and restored the garden, this had been one of the few plants still holding on to its original territory, which she decided to keep.

When the berries were ripe, Isobella was not allowed to touch. Ahes would harvest them along with leaves. She spent hours in the kitchen, boiling and reducing and straining until she had a dark tincture. This was decanted into small bottles which were kept in a hinged box lined with green velvet. It was kept on a high shelf and was strictly out of bounds. Now and then Ahes would take a bottle and wander out into the forest, leaving Isobella in charge of the cat. She would be gone for hours, sometimes a day or more, and would return far calmer than when she had left. As if she had found a release for her worries and anxieties, and all was well with the world.

Isobella was sitting in the sunshine on the bench under the witchhazel. She wore the patterned gingham dress Ahes had made for her yesterday. She had a twig with a nutshell attached on a piece of string. She made the shell dance across the empty space on the bench, humming to herself a tune of no particular composition. The cat, which she insisted on calling Tomas despite the fact Ahes pointed out the cat was a female, was pounce-ready at the end of the bench. With single minded focus, the cat watched the nut, and every now and then a paw would dart out, claw catching on the rough edge of the shell. Tomas would go in for the play-kill. Isobella would giggle, telling the cat she was silly. Taking offence, Tomas yawned, that skull-stretching cat gape, before hopping nimbly to the grass and stalking off amongst the onions.

Isobella was eight years old. Oh to be eight. So young and innocent of the heart break of the world. Ahes turned away from the kitchen window and went to the mirror by the door to inspect her features. She would be forty this year. There were creases around her eyes. Her hands were chapped and calloused. There were more white hairs in her tangled nest of hair than she cared to consider. She reached for her pipe resting on the little shelf below the mirror, then hesitated. It would not be enough this time.

Retreating to the shadows of the homely kitchen, filled with soft cushions and curtains, generous shelves carrying books and bottles of dried herbs and preserves over the years, she took down a book of fairy tales and set it on the kitchen table. Dragging a footstool across, she hopped up and brought down the wooden box, taking a half full bottle and replacing the box. She slipped the bottle into the pocket of her dress, slung her foraging bag over her shoulder, and picked up the book as she left the house.

Her long skirts rustled past the borders of herbs as she walked up the garden, the action releasing clouds of thyme perfume. She reached Isobella and crouched down. She stroked the girl's hair, righting a green ribbon that had come askew from running about in the woodland. "My little Bella," she cooed. "Here." She passed her the book.

Isobella took the book, gazing down at the cover. It was a favourite, she knew the tales by heart and didn't really need the book, but loved to look at the intricate illustrations, go through those words and stories. Imagine other places.

"You know where the food is inside. And you are to go to bed when it is dark if I am not back by then."

She looked up. "You are going into the deep forest?"

"Yes."

"May I come with you?"

Ahes smiled gently. "You know that it is not for little girls."

"But I'm eight now!"

"I know, and that is a very great age. But you should stay in the sun and play. Tomas will look after you." Ahes stretched up, feeling her knees crick. "I must go now."

Isobella stuck out her bottom lip in the start of a sulk, but to no effect. Ahes left by the garden gate and started into the forest on a trackless route. The girl looked back at the front cover of the book, then across to Tomas, who was crouched down between the green sentries of onion leaves, watching her. She never knew what mother did when she disappeared into the forest, only that she was distracted before, and when she returned she had found peace. For a time at least. Isobella put the book down on the bench. She wasn't a baby anymore. She was going to find out.

Ahes moved swiftly and without sound through a forest that was as familiar to her as her own skin. Isobella's legs were shorter and her tracking ability not as honed. She had not explored the forest as much and her own mental map of the land was not as widespread. It was some time before Isobella caught up with her mother, more out of good luck than cunning skill, and what she saw confused her.

She had not realised that other people lived in the forest. In truth, the world beyond their cottage, the garden, and the trees had not particularly troubled her. For the first time she found herself wondering if the forest ended and what might lie beyond it. Were there many other people? Of course there must be, for she had learned different languages from lands faraway. She had read history and stories. But places like France and Ireland had as much relevance to her as the fantastic worlds in her fairy books. Places she had assumed she never might go to.

Ahes was communing in the forest with another person. Isobella, nestled in the safe depths of the hawthorn thicket, carefully leaned forward to get a better view. What was happening? Ahes stood on her knees in the woodland litter of leaves and undergrowth. Her head craned back as she gazed off in the forest canopy. Her skirts flowed out around her like the great mass of an aged tree trunk. Protruding from one end of the skirts was a pair of the legs, from the other the torso of another person. A figure with short hair, a bulkier frame and a flat chest. A man, she guessed. He looked like the prince in her fairytale book. Although men usually rode horses or strode valiantly into danger. They didn't usually just lie about on the ground. This one was groaning as if in pain. Perhaps he had been attacked by a dragon. Mortally wounded. Ahes groaned. Perhaps she had been wounded too.

No. Isobella did not really understand what was happening, but her natural instincts told her that neither party were in pain or under duress. They wanted to be there. The act was reaching a culmination of sorts, the jerking movement increasing in pace and intensity. The man cried out in joy and Ahes dropped back on her haunches.

They were quiet for a few moments, catching their breath. The man raised himself on his elbows and looked up at Ahes. "Where have you been hiding yourself?"

It was difficult to see Ahes' face now that she no longer looked to the heavens. Her hair was loose and hung around her face. She didn't reply, but put her hand to her coat pockets. Will she take the bottle of tincture now? Isobella wondered. But no. A knife appeared, and before either Isobella or the man could quite comprehend the meaning, Ahes had lashed out and sliced open the man's throat. He looked intensely confused, his gaze moving from Ahes' face to the burbling outpouring of dark thick blood. His arms wobbled and he slumped back to the ground. Ahes wiped her knife on a clean patch of his shirt.

Horrified, Isobella slipped soundlessly into the background of the forest and hurried back to the forest, not quite sure what she would do when they two would meet again.

Ahes was gone several hours before she returned to the cottage. She had taken her time, digging a grave and disposing of the body, checking the pockets for any loose change. She had enough money to continue her subsistence lifestyle, but a little extra help would never be unwelcome. Her apron had been splashed with blood, so she burned it before completing her business and returning home.

It was late when she returned. There was a low fire burning. The cat slept in the rocking chair. Isobella was in bed, pretending to sleep, but as soon as Ahes walked in through the door, she could tell from the air that she had been seen. She could not ignore this. She would have to prepare a strategy in readiness for the morning.

It is a commonplace assumption that the desire of the mother is to protect the offspring from all the dreadful things in the world as long as possible. Just as it is the natural instinct of the murderer to avoid capture, and to deal with witnesses effectively. Where exactly Ahes lay within this puzzle was uncertain.

Ever since she had taken up residence within the depths of this ancient forest, she had sporadically taken the lives of men both young and old. Men who had wandered from the paths and found themselves in what they assumed was forgotten land, untouched and unseen by humans for decades. Sometimes she had to tempt one away from the path when she was needy and no one had strayed. In the last few years she had found that her allure was not as complete as it had been in the first springs of youth. Some declined her and walked on, something which she could not allow to pass. For who wanted talk of a sex-starved mad woman of the trees over a tankard at the village pub? She had been forced to hunt those ones down and exterminate them without first taking her fill. It had left her more dissatisfied than before.

The natural passage of time meant that nothing was ever the same. The same rules would apply to their household. In the twilight hours Ahes decided what would be done.

It started, as many things do, in the garden. Ahes had brought Isobella up to understand the garden, how to care for different plants, and what these plants could give back to them. But they'd never cared for the bushes to the edge of the garden, the ones with the black berries. That had always been Ahes' responsibility alone.

"The most important thing you must remember," Ahes explained as the two crouched beside the plants, "Is that you must never eat anything directly from the plant."

Isobella eyed the plant suspiciously. This had been a new thing this morning, to be told she was to learn of the secret of the garden. All horrors of yesterday were pushed to the back of her mind. Instead she was keen to find out what had been kept from her in the garden. She could be easily distracted. Her eyes ran over the deep green, and rather inoffensive looking leaves. There were green berries now, which she knew from having watched the seasons, would become an inky black.

"Why?"

Ahes pursed her lips. If she was going to raise this girl properly, she would have to be told everything. "Because it is full of toxins. Poison. The leaves, the roots, the berries. Everything. If you ate one of the leaves now, you would die."

Isobella gasped the childish gasp of surprise. "Is there no cure?"

"Only death."

"Why do we grow it, if it is so terrible?"

"Because perhaps one day there will be an emergency and we may need it."

"You cook with this."

Ahes smiled. "Yes, you have seen that I prepare a tincture from this. And we must be very careful with this. For if you take too much, it will kill you. But with just a drop it can do some very special things. Things to your experience of the world. But also in appearance. The Italians gave it a special name. Belladonna. It means beautiful woman."

"So I can become a beautiful woman?"

Ahes smiled lightly. "I think that will happen anyway. But with this you can also expand your mind."

For the next few weeks Isobella learned how to cultivate and care for the plant, how to keep it under control and to dispose of any parts that either from pruning or cooking, were no longer required. Thomas would certainly die if she ate any, and they did not want any to accidentally make it into their normal food chain.

But Ahes told her how some animals, such as rabbits and cows, could actually eat it with no ill effect. It was a mystery why this was.

They worked in the kitchen, preparing and slicing, boiling and straining to make fresh tincture. They filled small glass bottles with the strange liquid. The bottle lids had glass pipettes built in so that it could only be released drop by drop, for it was so important not to overdose.

It was a month after the death of a stranger that Ahes and Isobella went into the forest together. Tomas, not wishing to be left out of proceedings, followed them, slinking around the trees and occasionally stopping at the sound of an incautious mouse. Following no path, only Ahes' comprehensive mental map of the land, they came to a forest glade and sat among ferns and mossy stones.

Ahes took a bottle of tincture from her pocket. "Do not be afraid of what happens. This will open your mind. Show you unseen things."

Isobella reached for it. "Do I drink it?"

"No, no, no. Tilt back your head and keep your eyes open."

Tomas padded out into the glade and sat on her haunches to watch.

Two drops were applied, one to each eye. There was a splash of liquid and the world became blurred and washed out. Isobella began to blink furiously, an instinctive reaction. She hoped the sensation would soon wear off. She gazed across to the trees at the far side of the glade to settle her vision. They looked the same, in fact had anything changed? She had been expecting magic. She felt nervous, on edge, but that was all.

"How do you feel?"

"I don't know," she murmured. Her gaze shifted to where Ahes sat. Her mother was blurred. She blinked but she could not get her mother into focus. If anything, her vision was growing worse. "I am blind."

"Nonsense. I may be blurred, but I think far away you can still see. These effects will wear off. But look between the blurs. What can you see?" Ahes held Isobella's wrist, the tiny pulse belting frantically. Had they started this at too young an age? She had been sure to take a slightly watered down concoction. She watched as Isobella's pupils continued to dilate, until they could stretch no further. Deep, wide pools, like open windows onto the soul. With her dark hair and pale skin, the wide eyes created a character of childlike beauty. This was the effect the Italians had sought, that doe-like, animal-innocent eye.

Tomas mewed and approached them. Isobella watched the cat, growing all the more fuzzier as she grew closer. The cat stopped and regarded the child.

"This isn't magic," Isobella whispered, feeling frightened.

Tomas blinked. Tomas remained in place, watching with uncertainty. At the same time Tomas also turned and started to walk away. Two cats. One was so blurred she couldn't look at it, but the other was leaving.

"Tomas?" Isobella scrambled up and followed the cat.

Ahes and Tomas remained in the forest litter. They regarded one another as Isobella left. Ahes smiled. It was working. She got up and followed at a distance, to make sure no harm would come to Isobella.

The cat wound its shamanistic path around trees and undergrowth. Flowers shimmered out at Isobella as she passed by. They stumbled onto a small forest path, forgotten and neglected and hardly walked these days. Isobella circled on the spot. Tomas had disappeared.

In the distance walked a figure. He paused for a moment as the small child stumbled out of the undergrowth. He hadn't thought this part of the forest had been mapped or used for a long time. He should never have just listened to the local landowners. The rich who lived in large properties and employed their supposed social inferiors to walk the stretch of their estates. Nothing could beat proper local knowledge of the village folk. "Hello?" he called out. The girl continued to stagger around, almost drunkenly. "Are you all right?"

Isobella ceased in her circles, and remained shyly at the side of the path, gently swaying to unheard rhythms. There was a man walking along the path towards her. He had a leather satchel slung over his shoulders. Perhaps that was where Tomas had hidden. In his right hand he carried a long walking stick. It just looked like a fallen branch he had picked up from the forest floor. As he came closer he grew more indistinct. Her vision worsened.

"My goodness," the stranger breathed as he stopped in front of Isobella. The child gazed up at him, seeing precious little. Her eyes were amazing, both intensely beautiful and grotesquely melancholic at the same time. This was not natural. Was she afflicted by an eye condition, something that had damaged her sight? She had no iris, only black dark pools of pupil.

"Are you ill?"

I am not quite myself, Isobella thought, although she could not form the words.

She did not look that old. If she was a village girl, they may not have taught her English yet. He did not know any Welsh apart from some rudimentary greetings. "I, er..."

Isobella turned and started back into the woodland.

"Wait," he went after her, already haunted by her stare. "I don't think it's safe to go there if you can't see."

He stumbled into the forest, branches tearing at his clothes, pulling on his satchel. He pushed bramble creepers away with his stick. He tried to keep track of the girl. Coming around a large sprawling oak of many centuries, he came up short in front of a fully grown woman. She had waved, dark hair with silver threads. A feint scent of tobacco hung in the air, mixed with freshly cut wood and something else he couldn't identify.

"Have you seen a little girl?" he asked, catching his breath.

The woman smiled as if she were about to interact with an imbecile. She placed a hand gently on his wrist and shook her head, as if to tell him there was nothing to worry about. Without consciously making any move, he found himself lowering to the forest ground.

That summer there was much experimentation. Isobella often spent her days on another plain, not quite sure what was real, distorted or simply a hallucination. Her eyes fully dilated, and gasping she would stumble through the woodland. Tomas watched in distress from a distance. Three more men vanished.

Sometimes she would creep back after Ahes had dismissed her. From the cover of the undergrowth she would watch the mutual wrestling between Ahes and the strangers, and wonder if this was what one did to please a man. Throats were slit and knives were stabbed into chests. Was this what men needed? Isobella's fairytales only told of the shy, coy chasing; anguished time apart, unrequited love and lovers cruelly separated. When they joined, the culmination of their wishes, the story would end. It was a case of happily ever after, as a knowing laugh. For didn't everyone already know what that entailed?

Once every couple of months Ahes would leave the cottage and the forests. She wound away the few miles to the edge of a forest road. She had hidden her bicycle in a little dip, and with this she would complete the final distance to the village. She would purchase the necessities of life she was neither able to grow or create herself. The little market town supplied most of what she needed, and anything else could be sent for. She had collected letters from Brittany for a time, but with the death of her mother, the last of the meaningful connections died out. She had inherited far more than she expected, which she had invested with a local solicitor, not knowing what else to do with it. She had no need for fine clothes and objects, and for the most part money was meaningless in her life.

Yet it was one September afternoon when her shopping was completed that she heard snippets of unnerving conversation. Ahes sat outside one of the pubs, enjoying a tankard of ale and smoking a pipe. The men had long since learned to leave her alone; to not even make lewd comments under their breath whilst she was in town. Bouts of illnesses and stomach cramps after humiliations and insults had swiftly taught them the consequence of their actions. Local women gave her strange stares, half-shielded by shawls, and hurried on their way.

There was a boy who was missing. He'd been gone over three months. Last seen walking into the forest.

Ahes' expression remained as stone.

He'd been employed by the estate to properly map the lands. There was some disagreement between the estate and the government's forestry department over exactly who owned what. It would take longer now for the issue to be resolved, now that the cartographer had vanished, but new men were coming from London. There'd be a local with them to make certain they didn't get lost.

He was buried deep. No one would find him. She had made sure of that. But it was not the talk of the man, rather what he was doing, that concerned her.

"*Kac'h.*" It was the expletive that evening at the kitchen table. Isobella heard the harsh word, faded in sleep, and rolled over in bed, murmuring. Ahes waved her hand as if to brush sleep back over the child. "No matter," she muttered, looking through the other papers from the satchel. She had unfolded a large map on the table. The gossip was true. They were mapping out this land, and everything between the forestry village and the estate manor house was to be parcelled up and marked against a particular owner. Most of it was already in one camp or the other. There was debatable land to the north. Further south there was a tract that included their little dell which was historically common land, essentially long forgotten to the locals due to inaccessibility.

Her fingers curled sharply in fury, crumpling sections of the hand-drawn map. She would have to return to the town tomorrow and visit her solicitor. She needed to stake her claim now before another bought up the last patch, looking to extend their empire as far as they might go. She did not want anyone else setting foot on what she considered as her land. It was not how she had planned life, in truth the last she had expected was that she would be living in the middle of Wales. But things rarely went as one had hoped as a child. Once the tie with the fairy books was finally severed, the reality of life would come blundering one step at a time.

When Ahes had been a little girl she had said that nothing would persuade her to leave the beautiful Breton coast. When she married Patrick Donagh, she was certain she would be by his side for as long as she lived. What a strange route life had weaved for her. In the end she was not even able to live on the same land as her beloved.

From the lack of a child, the existence of so much good was overlooked and the relationship faltered. Patrick spent more time in the pub. Ahes spent more time alone wandering the coast and looking for she knew not what. Perhaps they might have found their way back to one another, but for the arrival of the third party. The Welsh had sailed into port.

A small Welsh fishing boat had taken on water during a particularly violent storm in the Irish Sea. Too far from home, it had headed for the Irish coast and moored at the town to make its repairs before heading home. This period left the small crew with time on their hands. One particular young Welshman, broad and dark haired, took to walking along the beach. One morning he heard strange singing in a language that was familiar and yet not completely comprehensible. Many words sounded similar, intelligible to his native Welsh, others were just nonsense. He found the singer, Ahes, crouched by a rock pool with her fingers dipped in the salty water. She looked up at the sound of his approach and something soundless snapped, like a crack of thunder. She was lost to his stare.

He spoke to her in Welsh, and he noted the recognition in her face. Whilst Breton and Welsh are distinct languages, there is certainly some mutual understanding possible, and their linguistic history is far more closely entwined than to that of the Irish.

Neither could quite explain, in any language, what happened that moment. They both understood the base urge, and as the man crouched down beside her to peer into the water, Ahes was sure she had just found the answer to a question she had not even asked. Her fingers filtered through sea water to brush against his hand. Then she was pulling him upon her in the sand in a flurry of movement and desire, words of passion as old as the ages whispered.

It continued for the month the ship was in dock. When she wasn't with him, her heart ached and her mind could not concentrate on anything. She was a lost soul. She barely saw or heard her husband. When the ship sailed back to Wales, she felt as though she would die in that moment, standing on the cliffs. The wind whipped right through her, and she knew what she had to do.

Packing her meagre belongings, she fled Ireland and travelled back across to the mainland of the United Kingdom, her goal set on the Welsh coastline. He had told her of his village, of the topography of the land, and she knew she would find him. She would be whole again. She walked for five days, and arrived exhausted in the little village, a stranger immediately noted by the locals. She walked the harbour, eventually met by the horrified stare of her beautiful Welshman. Her wonderful man who had returned home to continue his courting of the pretty village virgin. He had no need of mysterious exotic women, especially those who were already married. He swore and shouted at her, and even for the words she did not know, she could guess well enough the meaning from the tone in his voice and the look in her eye. Her heart was broken.

She wandered for weeks, a tramp and a vagrant on the landscape, not knowing what to do with herself. Her tears continued, but her mourning for the Welsh ceased as she realised it had been only lust. Fast burning, quickly extinguished lust. Beyond that the Irish boy still had her soul. She had made a terrible mistake, but these things could be made right. She wrote to him, longing and full of apology. Certain they could make things work. She received her answer. In no uncertain terms, she was never to set foot in Ireland again. She was dead to him.

She had lost everything.

She could not bear the sight of the sea. She walked in land, up the valleys and into the ancient woodlands, looking for a place to die. There was no point in the life of Ahes now. Far from any path or habitation, lost to the wilds of the forest, she came upon a crumbled stone ruin, with the overgrown remains of a garden. She sat beside the deadly nightshade and discovered a new meaning of life.

Ahes never did quite decide what it was exactly that drew those lonesome wandering men to Isobella. Once she had thought it was the doll princess-like stature of her childishness. A small pretty girl lost in the woods, appearing like a nymph. Disorientated. Oh, won't some fine knight rescue me? That and those unearthly eyes, enormous pools of blackness, great black holes that sucked everything in. But they never touched, and once distracted were easily taken by Ahes' womanly pleasures. Blood nourished the earth. Roots wrapped around carefully buried bones. Ahes felt stability settle in the atmosphere.

As the years passed, Isobella grew in height to match her mother, and eventually to overtake her in her late teens. She remained utterly innocent, and rather quite ignorant on some subjects. At least Ahes believed it to be so, never wishing to compete with her adoptive daughter for the carnal pleasures of men. She did not tell her the facts of life, certainly not for their own species, and assumed that when Isobella was finished in her role, luring the men to their deaths, she would roam mindlessly in the woods, hallucinating and day dreaming. She didn't know that Isobella hid and watched. Isobella had learned the art of observation through her quiet and isolated life in the woodlands, with only her mother and Tomas to talk to. And these days Tomas was old, and only cared for sleeping. Isobella's life lessons were finely gathered.

Ahes had run out of tobacco. The sugar jar was empty. She needed to check her mail. In the kitchen, she watched out of the window as Isobella tended the garden. She was picking peas, a pod for the basket, and another opened and deflowered quickly, the fresh green peas disappearing into Isobella's mouth. No matter how many she consumed, the evidence was always neatly dealt with, and when Ahes went outside there would never be any evidence of the loss.

Slinging her bag over her shoulder she stepped out into the sunlight. "I have to go for a while."

Isobella moved slightly.

She held up her hand. "Not that. I have to collect supplies. I will be back in a few hours."

"Can I?"

"No, no." She smiled, cupping her daughter's chin. She knew that it would be the same question. May she come to the village? No. Too many questions, Ahes knew. Nobody out in society knew of Isobella's existence and she intended to keep it that way. "There is nothing good out there. You stay here in the sunshine. I'll be back by dusk."

Ahes marched into the foliage, towards the bicycle she kept hidden. Isobella turned away, scowling at her shadow. Why would her mother never let her get out and see the world? There had to be more than this damned cottage. What of the castles and the great grassy plains she read of. What of the sea? She longed to hear the sound of the sea, but the coast was a subject Ahes rarely tolerated. Why did she spoil things like this? Isobella balled up her fists. Stupid mother.

Dusk fell but Ahes did not return. Isobella lit the oil lamp and sat by the kitchen window, watching a gentle coolness drift down amongst the trees. Tomas slept on a cushion by the fire. She read her book for a time, hung up some herbs for drying, then retreated to bed. She would talk to her mother tomorrow again about exploring the world.

Two days later Isobella realised that Ahes was not coming back. She did not know what had happened; only that it had never been this long, and something had changed. She had gone. There followed a week of rain and she stayed housebound and listless. She did not want to do anything. It was on the day that the rain stopped and the sun sparkled through water droplets on grass stems, that the strangers arrived.

Isobella had heard the sound of movement in the forest. She could tell from the volume, from the lack of thought, that it was human. She knew that Ahes never made so much noise, and could often appear unexpectedly at the cottage. But it had been so many days that Isobella wasn't thinking logically, and in any case perhaps Ahes was injured. It would explain why it had taken so long to return.

She went out into the garden and waited by the gate, certain that those sounds were coming in her direction. Her hearing was keen and it was some time before there was anything to see. Mildly curious, Tomas hopped up onto the stone wall and strolled down to Isobella. She stopped, stretched out her back whilst waving her rump in the air, and with a great yawn curled up to doze in the sun.

There were three people: two men and a woman. The woman and one of the men were much older than even Ahes. Both wore glasses and trotted and chattered quite blind to their surroundings before they caught sight of Isobella. They reminded her of the elderly couples in the fairy books. The old witch who baked children. The younger man walked with an awkward gait, slightly behind his elders. He wore dark clothing with bright buttons stitched in neat rows, and an odd hat. The clothes gave off a certain gravity but he appeared to be lacking in confidence behind the disguise. He did not have the conviction of his clothes.

Isobella found herself gripping the top of the gate tentatively. Tomas opened her eyes. No stranger had ever found the cottage before.

The strangers looked as perplexed to see Isobella as she did them. They slowed to a halt a safe distance from the cottage and regarded the long haired girl dressed in out of date clothing. The woman was the first to break out of the spell, raising a hand and giving her a guarded smile. *"Bore da!"* she called across cheerfully.

Bore da, didn't that mean good morning in the local language? Ahes had started to teach her some Welsh, but soon given up. Ahes could only speak a few phrases herself and had no inclination to master the tongue fluently. Everyone around here spoke English. Breton, French and English had been enough.

The strangers glanced at one another when Isobella didn't respond. The girl looked as though she'd never seen another human being in her life.

In truth Isobella had seen people, albeit not for long, and was aware the woman had spoken in Welsh to her. She was frozen in terror and bewilderment. What would Ahes say to her when she learned that strangers had been to their sanctuary? Slowly she raised her hand in reply. Perhaps she could encourage them to leave without getting any closer. "*Demat.*"

The older man furrowed his brow. "That's not Welsh, is it?" he asked in English.

The woman tutted. "If you'd bothered to keep your connections with this place, you'd know."

He stuck his hands in his waistcoat pockets. "We must look to the future. English is the way."

The woman pulled a face.

"Who is she?" the younger man whispered.

"I think that was Breton," the woman said. "It certainly wasn't French. You said Mrs Donagh came from Brittany originally, didn't you?"

"Yes, of course. She would have been raised in the local tongue..."

The woman ignored his prattle and took a step forward. "Do you speak English, my love?"

Tomas was up on all four paws, building to an aggressive stance. This did not bode well.

"Of course," Isobella replied. The words came easily. "You are lost?"

The youth sniggered.

"No, my dear," the woman boldly struck out to the cottage, tired of this male shyness keeping them back. Treat people as you would like to be treated. Her eyes widened as the black cat on the wall hissed at her before hopping down into the garden and disappearing into the foliage. "Not very friendly, is he?"

Isobella ignored the slight against the cat.

"We've come here to Ahes Donagh's cottage. This is it, isn't it? We've got things to sort out. Papers to collect."

Isobella stared at her blankly.

"This is Ahes Donagh's cottage?" she repeated.

"Yes, but she's not here just now. You will have to come back another day."

"Well, of course she's not..." the woman started incredulously, stuttering to a halt.

"We knew that Ahes' cottage was here," the older man explained. "She owned this section of land. I was under the impression she lived as a recluse..."

Isobella squinted at him.

"That is to say, you rather have us at a loss. We don't know who you are."

They waited for an introduction that did not come.

"I do not know you either."

"Of course, of course," he chortled. "Introductions, I believe. My name is Mr. Griffiths. I was Mrs Donagh's solicitor; I looked after her affairs and now her estate. This is Miss Rees, my secretary. And this is Constable Morgan, from the village."

The young man who lingered in the background doffed his hat to her then straightened awkwardly, blushing as he realised his action had been unnecessary and out of place.

Isobella nodded.

"I'm afraid we still don't know who you are. I don't believe I've seen you in the village. How did you know Mrs Donagh?"

"Ahes?"

"Yes, if you will."

She glanced across the faces, surprised they did not know. "She is my mother."

"Mother?" the old man blustered, looking across at his secretary. Miss Rees in her own turn grew concerned. "This is most unexpected," he continued. "I had no idea Mrs Donagh had any offspring. Do you have any papers to prove this?"

Miss Rees shook her head in disappointment and lowered her eyes. Any fool could tell from the way the young woman spoke, that she did not know. There were more pressing issues to be cleared up than legal documentation.

"Papers?" What did he mean? Perhaps the book of fairytales.

"Perhaps we should come inside."

"No." Her hands tightened on the top of the gate. "I told you, my mother's away at the moment. You'll have to come back when she's returned."

Miss Rees looked sad. "How old are you, my dear?"

"Eighteen."

"Perhaps we ought to go inside. We can explain there what's going on. This must be all very confusing for you." She gently put a hand to the gate, as if breaking a force, and the tension in Isobella's forearms relaxed.

Isobella stepped back. "Very well. We can wait for her together."

There was a light drizzle in the air and the wind blew. Isobella hugged one of her mother's best shawls around her and hulked down into herself. It was disconcerting being in such a wide open area. There were barely any trees to be had here. Instead there were cottages, not just as the one she'd grown up, but rows of uniform houses, architecture she'd only seen in books. And here was a grey, cold building with a turret. Ahes had always curled her lip at the suggestion of religion. Despite her distain, she was planted in the earth by the village church, to remain until the end of the world. There was a small engraved stone at the head of the plot where they had planted her. Mr Griffiths had been very quick to let Isobella know it hadn't been too expensive and the cost had been taken from the estate, as was only right.

Isobella stared at the words carved into stone. Was this really necessary for the earth to take back the body? Ahes had never gone to such trouble when she had buried her men. In fact it would have been virtually impossible to even have known they had ever been there. No, this stone wasn't here for Ahes. This was here for people who still lived. Isobella only had to close her eyes to know her mother had gone.

Miss Rees had carefully explained what had happened, with Mr Griffiths chirruping in with extra details. Ahes hadn't been looking where she had been going when she had come into the village on her bicycle. She'd appeared out of nowhere and straight into the path of a delivery truck coming around the corner. The village doctor said that she would have died on impact and would have felt no pain. They should take comfort in that.

Because Mr Griffiths had been unaware of any offspring, or any surviving relatives back in Brittany, the funeral had been arranged and completed within the week of her passing. He had understood that there was a husband back in Ireland, but his contacts in Ireland had informed him that the man in question had emigrated to South America a good few years ago and was most probably dead by now. Of course, it had been twenty years at least since Ahes left Ireland, he added, looking tentatively over the top of his spectacles at her.

"Over twenty years," he'd repeated. "You do understand what that means? And you're quite sure you're only eighteen?"

Isobella's understanding of her own age was the best she could offer, for there was no paperwork in the cottage to indicate her own existence. There was no birth certificate, and certainly no parish records indicating the birth. Ahes Donagh had always been a bit wild, Miss Rees thought. She could imagine her in a forest dell, giving birth in solitude, and keeping the child a secret to spite the world. And look at the mess Ahes left behind her. There was no will, no heir apparent until Isobella had surfaced, but she had nothing to prove it. Certainly the girl would need some kind of documentation, if only to find her own way in the world.

The drizzle turned to rain. Isobella pulled the shawl up to cover her head. She walked out of the churchyard, guided by the splatter of raindrops, and returned to Miss Rees' cottage. The low level of rain wasn't enough to put the locals off. They paused in clusters before being dispersed to fresh groupings, watching the stranger walk through the village. Isobella couldn't understand everything they said. Welsh was a language unto itself. It sounded familiar, like a long lost relation of Breton. There were certainly many words that she recognised. Some phrases even made sense. But it was like a transmission through heavy radio static, had she known at the time what such a thing was. It was impossible to follow a conversation.

Mr Griffiths had said that she could not stay in the cottage until the probate was resolved. Even after that, neither he nor Miss Rees were keen for her to return. They had discussions about her future when they thought she was out of earshot, making big plans. In the meantime she would stay with Miss Rees, who would tutor her in a number of subjects to get her up to a decent level before she could complete her education elsewhere.

In the realm of languages, Miss Rees had swiftly accepted she had nothing new to offer the girl other than Welsh, which she was teaching despite Mr Griffith's prediction that it was a dying language that wouldn't be in use fifty years from now. Nonsense, Miss Rees said. Then there was geography, history, mathematics and the sciences. Modern manners and society were other essentials Isobella was missing.

Mr Griffiths knew a woman who ran an admirable finishing school in London that she may eventually be able to go to. When she could behave like a proper lady, coupled with all those languages, she might get a nice little secretary job with the government before she got married. Isobella didn't see the need for a husband; certainly her own mother had managed without. She listened to their chatter over her future without comment, idly looking at the atlas without any proper comprehension of urbanisation, cities, streets and roads, and miles of human habitation long from the wilderness of her home.

Miss Rees was not quite as sold on the London suggestion. "It's a very big place," she started, glancing uncertainly at Isobella. The girl was sitting in the window sill watching the village go by. Or rather the village watched her, in particular the lads. She was the talk of the young men round here, and Miss Rees had been worried that Isobella might take the first one that came along, and waste all her potential. One saving grace was that she seemed to take no interest in them what so ever.

"She needs to see more of the world than just Ahes' ramshackle cottage."

"I know, but is this the time? The countryside is safer, especially with talk of another war."

"Nonsense," Mr Griffiths would laugh, puffing out his chest like a rooster. "Memory serves many a purpose, and one will be to keep people away from the road to war. No one in Europe wants to go through that again. Mr Chamberlain knows what he is at. He will keep us safe."

Miss Rees did not look so sure. "No good will come of that German."

"Hitler?"

She shook her head solemnly. "There's dark times ahead."

Mr Griffiths patted her arm. "Don't trouble yourself. All will be well."

Miss Rees was under the impression that Isobella did as instructed and never went back to the cottage. In truth she returned several times a week. If she was too long away it felt as though she couldn't breathe. She would rise late at night when she was sure Miss Rees had fallen into a deep sleep, occasionally helped along by a little herbal addition to her evening tea. Slipping from the cottage, she would skulk through the village and out to the country lanes. She'd quickly learned how to ride a bicycle, and once she'd passed the village edge she would hop onto the contraption and pedal for the forest edge. When the forest road petered out, she would hide the bike and walk the rest of the way to the cottage. She would spend a small handful of hours at home, leafing through books, playing with Tomas in the moonlight and tending to the garden. Sometimes she lit a small fire and would leave it smouldering alone to keep a little warmth in the hearth. Occasionally she would take a drop of tincture and visit other places in her mind's eye.

Tomas always refused to go to the village, hopping nimbly from her arms when she went to push him into the bicycle's basket. Isobella would stand forlornly for a moment, watching the cat saunter back into the forest. She envied her freedom. Then she would notice the growing dawn and realise she needed to get back.

As she approached the village, she hopped down from the bike and pushed it around a corner of the road. She almost collided with a young man, still sleepy from the early rise and away to a farm labouring job. They stumbled backwards from one another, the bike clattering against a cottage wall. He recognised her immediately, this Isobella Donagh that everyone was talking about. She'd lived a wild life in the woods, lacking in contact with ordinary folk. Some said she wasn't right in the head, for she always appeared distant and never seemed to know how to behave. Some of the lads he drank with said she'd be grand at getting down to the dirty, although how anyone knew this he wasn't sure, for Isobella Donagh didn't appear to have any friends, aside from Miss Rees, and certainly no sweetheart.

The talk was right. One could lose oneself in her eyes. It must have been the shadows of the early morning, but her eyes appeared to be especially large. He went to help her right the bike and their fingers brushed. Desire is a strange beast, for sometimes all it needs is a momentary glance or the briefest of touches. There would never be another equal for him.

Isobella put her hands back on the handlebars and looked at this strange lad with the round eyes and dark messy hair. He could only have been a few years older than she. Who was he? And why did he have to stare at her as if she were malformed? She nodded her thanks and passed him.

"Er, wait. Miss Donagh..." he turned, expecting her to pause and look back at him. She continued as if he hadn't spoken a word.

"Miss Donagh?" He hurried after her.

Isobella heard his footsteps, and realised he had been talking to her. She could never get used to that name. Miss Donagh. Ahes had never called her such a thing. Isobella stopped walking as the lad appeared back in her line of vision. She was feeling a little woozy from the after effects of the tincture, and really needed to rest her head.

"Er, Miss Donagh, I just wanted to say welcome to the village," he fumbled with his words as much as his cap, which he now had in his hands. Her soundlessness was disconcerting. "I'm Garreth, Garreth Jones, like. I just thought I'd say, given we've not spoken before."

For all the stares and talking about her, very few had tried to strike up much of a conversation. What a shame she needed to get to her bed now. She smiled tiredly at him.

"Miss Donagh?"

"My name is Isobella," she said quietly. "I have to get back before I am missed."

"Yes, of course." He watched her go, still revelling at her Welsh with a slight accent of the exotic. Where had she been out to at such an early hour? And a secret place also. She must have a lover already, he thought sadly, as though a lowly farm labourer had stood a chance before. He returned to his trek to work, her brief words on repeat in his memory.

She longed for the cottage, for the trees, for the wilderness. Her fingers curled around the lacy edging of the blanket and she hugged the fabric to her frame. She was a plant in the desert, suffocating and dying. She did not want to be here.

It was twilight. Tomas would be out and free, hunting mice, the moonlight glinting in her eyes. Isobella lay in the metropolis, in a room of sleeping bodies. Bodies that were disconnected from the earth and did not mind the city. They thrived in it. This was the dormitory of Madame Maurier's Finishing School for Young Ladies. It was a facade. Madame claimed she was French, but Isobella could hear behind the stilted accent and the occasional mis-conjugating of verbs that the woman was not native. She did not trust her. The suspicion was mutual, for a girl from Wales who spoke English with an odd French lilt, carrying an Irish family name and claiming an affinity with Brittany had to be hiding something. Indeed she was, for Isobella was thoroughbred Welsh, but that secret would always be hidden, even to herself.

From the first day, both Madame and the girls had felt uncomfortable around Isobella. She did not know how to behave with other young ladies and with groups of people in general. She was lost in London, overwhelmed by the streets. She stared at buildings of more than one storey as if they had just fallen from the moon. She had never dined in a restaurant or taken afternoon tea in a coffee house, cared nothing for clothes and owned only one hat, a parting gift from Miss Rees which she constantly forgot to take out with her. When she was alone she would sit in corners and murmur strange songs to herself, in Breton. It was an odd language which no one spoke and few were aware even existed. The young ladies tittered to themselves that it sounded like an over production of phlegm.

Miss Rees had informed Madame of Isobella's history, and that she needed preparing for the world now that her mother had gone and she must find her own way. Madame was determined that she could make a fine wife for a gentleman out of any girl passed into her hands. But there were days when Isobella was so vacant; she might have been talking to a wax figurine.

Isobella did not make friends. She did not know how to, and did not think to for she was most content with her own company. The girls thought she was snooty, and without reason for they also found her primitive and out of touch. That in itself would have been bad enough, but jealously within the pack instinct of gaggles of girls is a dangerous thing. The pianist for dance class could not take his eyes off the girl, to the point he would stumble over notes or miss his start point. Girls he had once flirted with were now ignored. The post boy always asked after Miss Donagh. She turned heads when she walked down the street. And she did not care one jot. What a fool!

Isobella clenched the blankets closer and tried to evoke the scent of the tree bark. Tried to remember the feel of dappled sunlight on her skin. She so wanted to be home. She curled up and dreamt of Wales, whilst at home the farm boy lay sleepless and wondered where the haunting forest girl had gone. Theirs had been but the briefest of meetings yet he was besotted. It had been a month since she had gone to London. There were plenty of other girls to distract him. He had lost his appetite for others. It was so stupid to lose one's head over someone one had only exchanged names with on a quiet morning.

Isobella endured the whispers, the side glances and the catty remarks. Female bitching was a new experience but the primitive nature of it was instinctively understood. She continued with the lessons, trying to learn as much as she could. With Ahes' death, her destiny had invariably changed and she had to learn how to cope in this world on her own. With the discovery of the cottage and her own existence, she couldn't hide any longer. After some months, the local magistrate had been persuaded to legally accept Isobella's existence, and a retrospective birth certificate was arranged. Probate took longer, but eventually the deeds of the house and land were passed into Isobella's name. The local lord of the manor hoped she might sell the land to him so that he could extend his country estate, but by the time the ownership issue was cleared from the lack of a will, Isobella was in London learning to be the lady her new small wealth demanded.

Morning assembly, which was a dramatic title for such a small gathering, started a little differently that day. Isobella had been at the school three months, and had learned the habits of all the regulars. This was not Madame Maurier's style at all. She was already in the room before the girls arrived, already slumped in the chair. She did not look well. Whether she was late or on time, Madame Maurier always took the stage alone. Today a grim man loitered behind her. Something terrible had happened.

"Ladies, please," Madame Maurier implored them to be quiet. "I have news that I must impart to you."

The gossiping levelled off, and best friends glanced at one another, trying to guess at what the exciting news would be.

"I'm sure that many you have noted the absence of our treasured pianist, Mr Forde, these past few days."

A girl sitting behind Isobella snorted to her friend. "I bet he's got one of the girls in the family way."

Madame Maurier shot her a look, not having heard the precise words, but certain they were most inappropriate at this time. "I have the unfortunate task of informing you ladies that Mr Forde is no longer with us..."

Emmeline, one of the pianist's greatest admirers, gasped out loud. "He's taken another job?"

Madame smiled wearily. "With the heavenly choirs, my dear child."

Uncertainty reigned in the room. The silent man stepped forward, clearly disappointed with Madame's handling of the matter. "May I introduce myself? My name is Inspector Ballard, and I have the sad duty to inform you that Mr Forde has passed on."

Emmeline burst into sobs. Glances were exchanged. One girl raised her hand. "Was it painless?"

Madame put a hand to her forehead. "Must we go over this ghastly business again?"

The inspector ignored her. "Sadly, no. I'm sorry to report that Mr Forde was murdered in this vicinity but two days ago. We found his body discarded in the undergrowth..."

Some girls started crying, one or two shrieked, but most began to chatter, already theorising and creating myths about the piano teacher and his death. He would become a legend of their year. Isobella sat quietly with her hands on her lap and stared down at her shoes.

"Ladies, there is a madman in the neighbourhood!" Madame cried out.

"I would not incite panic, and we do not know that," the inspector interrupted, feeling this was soon to be out of control. He dealt with petty thieves, jealous husbands who throttled their wives, gangs and the poor out on the look for a quick shilling. With a room full of well-to-do young women, equally excitable and hysterical, he felt out of his depth. "This may well have been a robbery gone wrong. We believe it happened late at night. Be assured we will catch this villain. In the meantime I would appreciate it if you ladies could be vigilant. Do not stay out late, and if you must go out, do not go alone..."

A girl called Harriet grasped Isobella's hand. "We shall look after one another, shan't we?"

"My ladies are trained to be respectable. None would be out so late," Madame protested.

"And if anyone knows the movements of Mr Ford over the last few days preceding his death, I would be grateful for any assistance you could provide." His eyes flicked over the array of young ladies. He doubted any of them would know anything useful, but the question had to be asked for the thoroughness of the report.

Emmeline raised her hand.

"Yes, Miss?"

"I...I," she choked. "I loved that man dearly."

A couple of girls close by started tittering. Madame waved a handkerchief in her direction then looked to the inspector. "A school girl crush, please do not concern yourself with it," she said quietly, quite certain that Emmeline's father would not want the girl mixed up in a murder enquiry. Especially one that had virtually solved itself, for it was certainly a thief. "Now ladies," she added with more volume to her voice. "Lessons are to be cancelled for this morning. If any of you do think you can help the inspector, you can let me know and I will contact him." She turned to the inspector. "This terrible news has clearly upset them. I think we need this morning to regain our balance."

"Well, I..."

Madame had certainly found her balance, and quickly. She took the inspector by the arm, like the greatest hostess, gently but firmly manhandling the unwanted guest from the party. "I'll let you know if they think of anything, but I'm sure not one of them has any notion of what may have happened."

Isobella watched the inspector leave, as she toyed with the crystal pedant around her neck. It was a little trinket she'd picked up on a weekend shopping trip with Harriet. A neat little vial that could hold a few drops of whatever liquid one desired.

"It really is ghastly." Harriet was the friend who had latched onto Isobella quickly. Harriet was an awkward girl, awfully keen to make friends, yet she emitted some undetectable sound that most found unappealing. She had the air of an over-keen fool. With the arrival of Isobella she had taken advantage of another awkward soul who struggled to fit in and she was quite happy to ignore Isobella's regular apathy, only so pleased not to be avoided. "How dreadful his last moments must have been."

Dreadful indeed.

It was only a few days before the tears started again. There were gasps, handkerchiefs clutched tightly in white knuckles. Girls huddled together and shared frightened looks. A few started to sob. Isobella barely reacted. Perhaps she did not comprehend just how terrible this could be, for she had only been in society the slightest of times. Barely a year.

She doubted it could have been such a great surprise for everyone, for they did not usually listen to the radio at this time in the morning. Madame had insisted that lessons be paused promptly at eleven in the morning and all girls were to gather in the assembly room. The young ladies primly sat down on the chairs. Tutors loitered at the back of the room. There was to be an important announcement. Isobella wondered what Madame was about to tell them, but instead the radio was turned on. It was Madame's own wireless, a particularly good set with exceptional sound quality that had been brought into the room for the occasion.

And so that morning, with autumn ever approaching, they listened tentatively as the country's leader, Neville Chamberlain, announced the news that everyone had hoped would never come. For surely, after the Great War, no one would ever wish to go in for a second round.

"I have to tell you now that no such undertaking has been received, and that consequently this country is at war with Germany..."

Some of the girls broke out into sobbing. Some had sweethearts who would be the right age for calling up. Brothers who could provide good fighting fodder. Isobella held her hands in her lap and looked around the room. So quickly Mr Forde was forgotten as the new tragedy lurched up. No one would miss a man killed in the back streets anymore.

The tutors were muttering between themselves. Everything people had based assumptions for their futures on had just been pushed over. Not just the hopes for ten years' time, but in a year, a month, next week. No one was quite sure what they ought to do even when the broadcast was over and they were left in no doubt that Britain had just signed on for another war.

Madame was pale. She looked over at her assistant. "I just don't know how much longer the school can continue," she spoke, her voice barely audible. Most were too involved in personal tragedies and fear to hear, but Isobella noted the comment. Perhaps she would be able to break free from this school sooner than she had hoped.

The English mistress clapped her hands together, noting that Madame seemed too flustered to take control. "Ladies, we are at war," she announced as the voices and chatter dropped to a murmur. "I realise this is a frightful shock for you all, but I think you will all agree that we will not let this interrupt our routine. Life shall continue and we will not allow the enemy the satisfaction of changing a thing..."

Already the enemy.

"...I suggest we return to our classes."

Numb in thought, and not knowing what else was to be done, they returned to class. No one could concentrate. People were burning to talk, or to contact loved ones, anything but to sit and pretend to be interested in what Shakespeare had to say about love this time around. At lunchtime it was decided they could take the rest of the day off from their studies, to digest the news, write letters, send telegrams and make calls – for the fortunate ones who had telephones installed in the family homes. But they were told they shouldn't worry. Nothing would beat the British spirit.

Isobella had no one to call. Although it stated British on her passport and papers, for want of anything to write to acknowledge the existence of a young woman overlooked by society for eighteen years, she did not know if she could consider herself of this ilk. Her mother had been French Breton. Her father was an unknown entity, although in the papers from the cottage, Isobella had found information about Ahes' husband, a Donagh who had given his name to both of them. Ahes had been married? It had been a shock when she'd first seen the marriage certificate. Mr Griffiths had assured her that it was true. Mr Donagh was an Irishman, possibly dead, for the last that had been heard of him, he had immigrated to South America. And that had been years past. So Isobella was a product of French Breton and Irish, so she told herself, and had little to do with this strange land she found herself within just now. Just whose side was she supposed to take in a war that felt as though it was on the brink of consuming the world?

She had sat on the edge of her bed for an hour, staring blankly at the wall and wondering where she ought to turn to, if she should be concerned about a certain people or a specific piece of land. Beyond the cottage, the woods, and Tomas, nothing else seemed to matter. And that little world seemed like a universe away from where she was. She touched the little vial of tincture that hung around her neck. It was reassuring to feel its sharp form against her fingertips and know that there was sufficient liquid in there should she need it.

At four o'clock she picked up her coat and made to leave the building. Harriet caught her in the corridor, linking arms. She already had her jacket on, as if she had known Isobella's plans and had simply been waiting.

"It's terrible, I still can't believe it," Harriet was saying as they walked down the staircase. "I don't think I will ever be able to attend another morning assembly. There's always such dreadful news. First Mr Forde, and now this."

Isobella murmured some meaningless agreement as they opened the front doors and stepped out into London. They were met by fresh air and a strange buzz in the atmosphere. People seemed to be rushing although they weren't quite sure where to or for what purpose. Only that war had been declared, and one ought to be doing something other than the daily grind, surely?

A figure darted forward to the young women. He had been loitering by the iron railings, sedentary and questionably awake. He had sprung to life as they had appeared, stepping up to Isobella's side. "Evening, ladies," he doffed his hat towards them.

"Alfred," Harriet spoke, leaning around Isobella. She hadn't expected to meet their local postman here so late in the afternoon. It was odd to see him out of his uniform and in a suit. He always had a twinkle in his eye, but today it was joined by something else. A sort of earnest desperation to be heard. "Isn't it awful news?"

"About time too if you ask me," he responded boldly, puffing out his chest like a little robin and daring to glance at Isobella. She didn't appear to have acknowledged him although all three had naturally fallen in to step. "Can't have those Jerries going about thinking they own the world. We'll show 'em what for..." he faltered, running out of bravado clichés. His Adam's apple bobbed nervously in his throat. "You ladies wouldn't care to join me for tea at Lyon's just now, would you?"

50

Normally the difference in class, certainly between Alfred and Harriet would have made the notion unthinkable. Even in the space of a few hours war had shook up people's ideas of decency. Harriet was thrilled by the idea. Isobella looked blank.

"I don't..." Isobella started just as Harriet declared loudly that they would love to go. Us Brits had to stick together, didn't we? Isobella found herself smiling weakly, her words unheard as Alfred beamed, linking with her free arm to escort them to the coffee house. And so the three of them trotted off down the pavement like a ridiculously jovial trio strolling straight out of a polite gentle operetta.

The coffee house was heaving when they arrived, but there was a little table at the back wedged in-between two parties of middle aged ladies caught in horrified gossip. There were only two chairs, which Alfred gallantly allowed the girls to take whilst he went in search of a third. Harriet was caught up in the buzz of it all, catching the attention of a waitress and ordering tea and scones. Alfred soon rejoined them; laughing that all there had been was a little stool that looked better suited to a milking parlour. He folded his bony long legs under the table and settled himself as the waitress brought their order. The table seemed a little too high now for him, giving him the look of their over grown and very strange son.

It was as Harriet was pouring out the tea that Alfred made his abrupt announcement.

"First thing tomorrow, I'm signing up."

Isobella watched the steam curl up off the surface of her tea, unaware of what he was referring to.

Harriet gasped and dropped the teapot rather heavily back on the table. "But aren't you afraid?"

"A man's got to do his bit for king and country," Alfred replied to Harriet's comment, whilst all the time looking to Isobella for a reaction.

"You're going to join the army," Isobella said, still looking at her teacup.

"Too right. Show 'em what's for. We'll be done by Christmas."

"But you must be nervous. Going to war. It's terribly dangerous."

"I'm not afraid."

Life expectancy was not good for soldiers. Isobella had read enough history to understand that much. Why anyone would want to sign up for an abstract concept such as country or religion was beyond her. The threat of death would put anyone off, surely? But when she now looked over at Alfred and examined his face closely, she saw his expression light up with joy. He really wanted to do this. To take on death. Was that what men wanted? She thought back on the men Ahes had taken in the forest. Such joy and then death.

"Miss Donagh?"

Her focus returned to the table and she realised some time had passed. Harriet and Alfred looked expectantly at her. They were waiting for something, but she didn't know what. "I'm sorry," she offered feebly. "I was lost in my thoughts."

"Don't you worry about old Alfred," their postman beamed at her, making the wrong assumptions. "I'll be right. But Miss Donagh, as I was asking, might I make the presumption and write to you whilst I'm away?"

Write to her? Why would anyone want to do that? She supposed him being a postman, letters were his business, and he was keen for the ladies of the finishing school to continue their connection. It wouldn't hurt. She managed a smile. "Why not?"

The war changed a lot of things in London society. Shortly after the declaration of war Alfred along with blossoming troops of other eager young men left their jobs and signed up. They disappeared to training camps, to secrets, to deployment, and for many, to a certain death. Madame Maurier's Finishing School only lasted six more months. Between girls eager to get to family country estates, and others wanting to get married or take up gainful employment to help the war effort, hardly anyone was interested in improving one's manners. Suddenly there were more important things in life. This new generation was filled with an intensity to live life in a week.

Isobella had left the school a couple of months after war was declared. She had remained in London, a choice that surprised even herself. Suddenly the desire to flee to the woods was put on ice as the temptation to gain experience in the wider world and earn some money took precedent. On account of her languages, she easily got a job with the Ministry of Defence as a translator. She was never told where the snippets of text had come from or what the context was. Paper hit her desk and she was to put it into English and pass it on to her supervisor. It was only French to begin with, but as word got through the system that Breton was also available in London, the Celtic tongue made a greater appearance. Whoever was penning these notes obviously felt some things travelled better in Breton.

She did not mix a lot at the office. Across the corridor from Isobella's office there was a girl whose father had been Italian. Both girls were oddities in different ways, and with multicultural roots, they naturally levitated to one another. The girl, Rosa, taught Isobella her mother tongue. Isobella picked up languages quickly, already having four under her belt, and it was a comfort for Rosa to have someone to talk to in the old language. The supervisor, who only spoke English and schoolboy French, would look sternly at the women when they arrived to work speaking *Italiano* in the corridor. Once separated, he would try not to be too obvious in his adoration for Isobella. At home in bed beside his sleeping wife, he was plagued by strange dreams of the big-eyed girl.

Harriet, the self-imposed friend from finishing school had swiftly followed Isobella out of education and into the work place. She had hoped they could work together but it was quickly noted that her linguistic skills weren't up to scratch and she didn't make the cut. She took a position in the typing pool at an office down the road and listened with wide-eyed innocence to the tales the officials and civil servants told. All in the name of the war effort.

Isobella received a steady flow of letters from Alfred in scratchy handwriting and composed in poor spelling. She would read them once over breakfast before leaving them unanswered on a shelf in her room. It did not occur to her that she ought to write back. After the first three or four, he mentioned worries that his letters might not be getting through. Or perhaps her letters were lost in the post. When subtle hints fell short, he asked her outright if she intended to reply. A few kind words would help keep his spirits up. She was disinclined but the letters did not cease, so she would occasionally send a postcard. She made a thoughtless and irregular penpal, but her obligations were short lived as Alfred was killed outright in a bombing raid in the first year of the war. She received a note shortly after from his mother informing her of the funeral and that although they had never met it would be good to meet her son's sweetheart. Sweetheart? Isobella had thrown the note out. Better for the woman to believe a lie than to break the truth to her. She promptly moved digs without leaving a forwarding address so that the entire sorry episode might be forgotten.

The bombing in London started in earnest. Most nights the chilling wail of the air raid siren would set off somewhere in the city. The skies would be lit up with fires and searchlights, filled with the ominous hum of enemy aircraft. If you were close enough to where a bomb fell, you could feel the very earth move beneath your feet.

At first Isobella followed her fellow lodger neighbours down to the air raid shelter simply out of formality. That was what everyone did, so she followed suit without thought. For some weeks it felt like a waste of effort, crammed in with those sweating, nervous bodies, waiting for the all clear that they were safe to come back out. She would find herself a dark corner, ignore the comforting words strangers tried to caress her with, and close her eyes. She would think of the crisp air of the forest. The dappled sunlight falling between the leaves. The sound of the wind moving through the tree tops. Bird song at dusk. The farm labourer's eyes.

One night, when they crawled shaking from the bomb shelter, they came out into a very different world from the one they had fled. Their neighbourhood had taken a direct hit. The street was covered in rubble. Air raid wardens were helping the fire crew trying to put out the fires. Shattered glass from a window was spread beside the remains of a tree. A pram crushed by falling masonry crumpled and motionless in the debris. A hole steamed where the neighbouring house had once been. The air was thick and grimy. It felt as though she was breathing in black soot. Her skin prickled against the flickering light of the fires, the orange heat reaching towards flesh. She numbly clambered her way across the piles of rubble to her home.

Half of the lodging house had been demolished with that hit. In the background, drowned out and not registering, Isobella could hear the forlorn cries of her neighbours. Clutching her handbag, wearing her autumn coat and bright green dress, she stared up at her home. Her side of the building had simply disappeared. Her room was no more. Her belongings burned to nothing. Her box of tinctures. Isobella dropped to her knees, distraught, and let out a mournful scream. A neighbour walked past and patted her shoulders, assuming the cries were for the landlady who had been far too stubborn to ever go down into the shelter.

In her bag she had a handful of vials, which ought to see her through a couple of years. But there had been decades' worth of tincture in that box. Not only that, but the box itself had been a treasure. A connection to her dead mother. Isobella had precious few possessions in this world. People were always surprised by how little came with her when she moved to a new abode. It was though a floodgate had been opened within her, and she cried sooty tears for her lost vials, for her lost mother, for things she could not put into words but felt so incredibly deeply.

The next day she arrived at the office with her hair a bird's nest, dark rings under her eyes and smut on her dress. She had spent the night helping the relief effort, moving rubble. Most hoped they would find the landlady alive, although their hopes were dashed a couple of hours into the work when her limp body was recovered. Isobella continued, hoping to find something of her life. All she recovered was a singed book of fairytales she'd brought with her from Wales. The box was lost.

With her handbag and fairytale book deposited on her desk, she'd dropped into her chair and stared blankly at the wall. She didn't know what to do. She had an increasing desperate need for the tincture, but as unworldly as Isobella was, she understood that it was not something one did in public.

Someone went for the office manager, who promptly arrived and ordered sweet tea to be arranged. It was the perfect opportunity to comfort the girl, have an arm around her unresponsive shoulders and snuggle up to her. Through the soot and burnt homes, sweat and terror, he could smell Isobella's underlying natural scent. It was intoxicating at this vicinity and he struggled to keep his hands just to her shoulders.

Rosa appeared in the doorway. She'd heard about the bombing raid at Isobella's street and the moment she had looked in the office she knew she had to get her friend out of there. "Her home has been destroyed," she spoke loudly with a terse undertone of impatience.

The office manager jumped. These Italians were always so brusque. "How terrible for you," he said, looking back to Isobella. "Where will you stay?" They had a spare room at home, intended for a child that never came. If she were to stay there, and his wife sleeping so deeply at night...

"She's going to stay with me," Rosa interrupted, as if reading his thoughts. Not even a fantasy should be allowed to go that far. "I don't think Isobella can work today. I'm going to take her home now."

He gave her a sour look. So much for neighbouring bedrooms. "Very well." He stood up, straightening his tie. "I'll see you both back at work tomorrow."

As they were walking down the street in the direction of Rosa's home, the girl burst out laughing. "My god, that man will take any chance." She looked over at Isobella. "You've got to be careful. Men always want to take advantage."

Isobella looked at her quizzically.

Rosa just shook her head in amusement. "My friend, where did you grow up? A cave?"

It was close enough. Isobella didn't illuminate her on her childhood or her strange parentage, but followed Rosa through the streets of London. Rose had found a little gem of a lodging room, with a bed and a settee. Certainly enough space for the two girls to share until Isobella managed to find somewhere new to rent.

"Bathroom's last door on the right," Rosa added, hanging off the doorframe and pointing outside of the room. "You sure you'll be okay tonight?"

Isobella looked up and smiled wanly. Rosa was seeing a Canadian airman. The evening date had already been prearranged, but she was looking to see him earlier in the day as well. There was excited anticipation in those eyes. "Of course. Say hello to Larry from me."

After Rosa had gone Isobella went and took a bath. Her dirty clothes were shed, strewn over the bathroom floor like the rubble from last night. She closed her eyes and lay back in the tepid water. What to do now?

She had a vial in the bathroom with her. She knew that she would have to use the tincture sparingly as she was now trapped with a limited supply until she could next travel to Wales and get a fresh batch made up. Before that she'd have to acquire some suitable bottles and a case to hold them. Still, it had been a very trying forty eight hours. A couple of drops and the vial would still be virtually full. She stared at the ceiling and let out a gasp as a drop was poured into each eye. Her soul lunged up from her chest and the colours broke apart from the light and swirled across the ceiling. An excited sense of anticipation flooded through her.

As the natural sunlight was fading from the sky, Isobella stood naked in Rosa's room, flicking through the contents of her wardrobe. She selected a deep purple dress, clean underwear to borrow, and got dressed. Slipping her feet into her freshly scrubbed shoes, the remnants of brew pulsing in her veins, she went out to the West End.

She wandered for an hour through the rush of people. Chatter burbled out from the shadows, scents coming from restaurants, couples determined to enjoy themselves to spite the war. They would not be stopped. This could all be the last chance. She felt jubilant, so as nothing would stop her, until the air raid sirens set off again. There was a pause, a collective intake of breath, then the rush of bodies changed direction and intention. People knew where they needed to go. Isobella stood in the middle of the road, numbly looking around her. She had never been in a strange place during an air raid. What was one supposed to do?

"You can't stand out waiting for the bombs, my darling."

Strong hands took her by the shoulders and hurried her down the street. She looked around to see a man with a pencil thin moustache and striped suit hurrying her towards the underground. So many people sheltered in the stations during the raids. The underground covered all of central London, a lifeline to the city. Why had she not thought of this before? As they reached the entrance, the sirens on full alert and the beams searching the cloudy skies, they joined the last groups of people headed for shelter. Heat and noise belched up from under belly. The stranger clutched her closer as they joined the others, as if to mark out possession.

"My, you are a pretty one," he whispered to her ear, his hot breath creating an air current that unsettled loose strands of hair by her face. "You and I should get better acquainted down there in the dark."

He took her hand and started to pull her to the underground. Isobella was naive but some things she understood. The heat and terror from down there felt too intense. She couldn't be there, to be groped by anonymous hands, to be pressed between sweaty bodies, to listen to the disembodied sobs. She slipped her hand free and ran down the street, stopping by a lamppost to look back. Most had gone underground, but he stayed out, watching her with a wry smile. "It's like that, is it?"

Isobella hurried away on a cloud of euphoria. Stumbling down a side street, she skipped to the end, reaching another junction and a road of half ruined buildings. Her heart beat fast in her chest. Pressing her back against the wall, she took a vial from her handbag and with a tilted head, fed her eyes. Colour exploded out of the sky. Jet streams from bombers warped and throbbed with sound. Pearls of moonlight pattered down through the heavens to earth.

His breathing was heavy as he caught up with her. She played a merry game. Reaching across, he took her shoulder and pulled her around to him. Her hair had come loose in the chase, like black silk tumbling around her face. Her eyes seemed to be abnormally large in the moonlight, hypnotic. Were he not so drunk on desire he might have taken a step back. "My god," he breathed. "You are something."

She took his hand and pulled him into one of the ruined buildings. Her feet managed to find purchase on the terrain without stumbling. He dumbly followed, thinking his luck was in this evening. Perhaps she was a foreigner, for he hadn't heard her speak a word. But there was an understanding between a man and a woman that was ancient and born long before language. "You can't wait for the featherbed, can you?" he joked, bravado to cover the fact that it was starting to dawn on him she might not be as inexperienced as he had first assumed.

"Like it a bit rough?" he asked as she brought him to his knees amongst the rubble. Still she said nothing. Her eyes were great pools of darkness, the pupils full of desire. He unbuckled his belt as she pushed him back against the dusty ground.

"Careful now, this isn't a cheap suit. I'll have you..." he groaned out as she mounted him. What she lacked in conversation she more than made up for in other ways. He would have preferred to see a little more flesh before they got to this stage, but with the endorphins pumping through his system; it didn't seem to matter just now.

Isobella arched her back and looked up to the moon creeping out from behind the clouds. She could feel he was close to climax. Somewhere in the distance bombs started to fall. The man beneath her groaned with ecstasy. She reached in her handbag and pulled out her ivory inlaid letter opener. He opened his eyes to look at her one last time before he came. Isobella smiled and slit his throat.

"These newspapers write such nonsense," Rosa grumbled, flicking ash from her cigarette out of the window. A slight breeze blew some of the smoke back into the room. Sunlight filtered through the glass pane. Patterns of light and shadow created from the tape criss crossing over the window lay upon the floor. The familiar crinkle of paper as Rosa turned the page. Outside came the sound of voices, wreckage crews clearing the street of rubble. Rosa had been lucky. Her lodgings hadn't been hit but the other side of the street was gone.

Isobella had been living in her new lodgings for over eight months, but the women would still gather at Rosa's rooms regularly to talk. They saw each other most days at work, but it wasn't the same at the office. There were always people trying to listen in, or others bringing yet more translations. And if it wasn't work, then the manager was simpering around Isobella. They might try and talk in Italian, if only to get some privacy, but that always got people's backs up. As if they weren't quite to be trusted with the war effort. They learned to keep their heads down at work and save the socialising for later.

She wasn't in a particularly talkative mood today. Rosa was sitting on the window sill. Isobella lay on her back on the little settee as if she were a patient come to see the psychiatrist. She gazed up at the stained ceiling.

"They're making a joke out of it all," Rosa continued. "Saying a woman is behind it all, although they are laughing because they don't really think a woman could be capable. I wouldn't want to think that a woman could do such terrible things. But this war... I don't know. It seems to bring out the best and the worst."

Isobella's brow furrowed. "What are you talking about?"

There was a loud crinkling of paper as newspaper was folded. "You must have heard about it; how could you not?" Rosa protested. "Ripper Jill? Well, it's the name this stupid journalist is using."

"Who is she?"

Rosa tutted. "She doesn't exist."

She sat up and looked across to her friend. "I don't understand. Is this a novel you're reading?"

"No. It's just a string of murders. You've heard about it, these men found with their throats slit? They are joking that it's the next Jack the Ripper, except that it must be a woman this time because all the victims have been men."

"Oh, those murders."

"I don't see how a woman could overpower all those men. It's just thieves if you ask me. Although..." she paused, stubbing her cigarette out before leaning forward. "The last one was an airman, you know. Claude told me something about it that they didn't put in the newspapers."

Isobella felt her pulse increase. "Claude knew him?"

"No. He'd only heard of him. They're at the same base, but he didn't really know him," Rosa spoke of her Canadian fiancé. "But he heard that when they found him, he wasn't properly dressed." Her eyes widened with innuendo.

"He wasn't in uniform?"

"Isobella, don't be so naive. His trousers were round his knees. As if he'd been involved in nigh time pursuits." She wiggled her eyebrows meaningfully. "There's been six of these cases reported in the papers. And I bet those are the only ones that they've connected. There's probably more. With all this bombing it's easy to lose track of the bodies."

Isobella turned away and lay back on the sofa. "Must we talk about these things?"

"I suppose not." Rosa held out her hand and tilted it this way and that, watching the diamond sparkle. "Johnny was asking after you again. He's always asking Claude about you."

She closed her eyes.

"Why not come out to dinner with us? We can make a foursome. It's not like you have any other steady sweetheart."

"I can't."

"Why not? It'll be fun."

"I've got some leave coming up. I'm going back home."

"To Wales?" Rosa broke out into a wide grin. "I knew it. You have someone back there. How did he stay out of the conscription? Doing important work for the country?"

Isobella didn't answer. Let her believe it if she wanted to. Perhaps she would stop asking about Johnny. She'd never had a sweetheart, in truth she didn't understand why people bothered. The mere suggestion of someone back in Wales made her think of the farm labourer: the quiet man with the round eyes. He probably wouldn't be there. He had been young and fit enough to be called up, and they would have replaced him with one of the land girls. He could be anywhere in the world now.

She needed to get back to the forest, which she hadn't seen for years. Most pressing was the fact that she had precious little of her tincture left, and it was a good time of the year to harvest the deadly nightshade to make a fresh batch. She had managed to replace the glass vials from a bombed out chemist, and now had more little bottles than she'd originally started with. She had found a couple of second hand cases in an antique dealer's that would contain and protect her bottles. All that was required was something to pour into them. She needed to return home.

The next week saw Isobella leaving London and making the long journey back to Wales. She started out on a mainline train, changing onto progressively more local and slower routes until she felt the air change. She could hear the very call of her forest. Here in the open countryside it felt almost as if the war had never happened. There were no streets of rubble, no half-destroyed buildings, no fires and sirens, no walking wounded and sobbing children. Yet no corner had been completely untouched, and even in rural areas changes could be seen. Where there once had been a predominantly male work force in the fields, the majority were women, dressed in their cord trousers, working shirts and brightly coloured headscarves. At strategic positions concrete bunkers had been constructed, covering points such as bridges and entrances to villages, should an invasion ever happen. The windows at the train station were taped up, just like the London windows. Piles of sandbags waited to prove protection against blasts. Yet it was preparation for a war that hadn't happened in their sphere. The people she passed by looked healthier here, well fed. They did not carry the gaunt look of the long suffering city folk. There was the bounty of the farms and fresh produce, and people could sleep through the nights.

Before heading out to the forest, Isobella thought she would pay a visit to Miss Rees. She walked through the village, catching locals' stares. There was a moment or two when people wondered who this well dressed woman was in her deep purple hat and well-cut coat, before the memory clicked. It was the same stunning face. The strange girl from the forest, Ahes Donagh's daughter. She had grown up into a well-to-do lady.

There was a man on crutches coming down the lane towards her. His body shadowed back into itself, and she quickly noticed that his left leg was missing from the knee down. No more use for the war effort, he would have been discharged and sent home. He paused in his swinging gait as he saw her feet first, and raised his head.

Isobella's breath caught in her throat as their eyes met. The labourer with those intense round eyes, now haunted by things that could not be unseen. His once pure dark hair was woven with white strands. He had aged more than the few years since they had last seen one another. She was so surprised by his appearance that her memory returned to the early morning when they had first almost collided. "Garreth Jones," she whispered his name.

A faint smile touched the corner of his mouth. "Miss Donagh. You're looking very smart."

"Out of place for this village," a sour voice added in Welsh.

They both looked across the street to a young woman with tight blonde curls and a stained dress straining at the seams. Elbows reddened from hard work and a wriggling baby in her arms. She looked angrily at Isobella. The baby whined and twisted, holding its arms out to Garreth. It stared at him imploringly with large round eyes.

"Excuse me, I have to visit Miss Rees," Isobella spoke, her Welsh fluent but still with that quaint accented lilt. "It was nice to see you again."

With a curt nod she stepped around him and hurried up the lane, grateful to have Miss Rees' cottage in sight. These three years seemed like decades. How the village had flown on through its life whilst she had been gone. She had not been missed. She knew then that she could not stay.

It had only been a sparse number of years, but Miss Rees appeared to have aged decades. It was unclear what could have led to such a change, certainly not the natural passing of time, and whilst there was a war and rationing, in the countryside people were still relatively well fed and usually far enough away from the bombings to have any concerns. The spark seemed to have gone from Miss Rees, and she had grown into a frail old lady. Her world had very much reduced to the village, and the happenings of the wider world troubled and frightened her however hypothetical to her day-to-day life they were. Humankind had found itself in a very dark place.

She was happy to see Isobella again, and to see that something had gone right in London. Although still a little distant from regular society, she at least looked the part of a civilised lady, and was getting on in life with work and learning. Perhaps the war had even afforded her some advantages. With the men away fighting, there was more work open to women, and likewise more work created to aid the war effort. She was pleased to hear that Isobella was able to put those languages to good use.

Miss Rees insisted that she stay for supper, and was keen for her to stay at the cottage whilst she was visiting Wales. Politely but firmly, Isobella extracted herself from that invitation. Unperturbed, she left at dusk and headed out to the forests with her bag. She needed to return to her childhood home.

At first she had wondered if she had lost some of her senses. It was strange to be away from the noise and so many people, but with the blackouts for the Blitz, her eyes could happily still cope with the darkness. Memories flooded back as she walked familiar pathways. It was almost as if she had never left.

She had known that the cottage would be different. No one had lived there for three years. The garden was overgrown, noticeable even in the twilight, and the cottage looked dank and cold, forgotten. Isobella unlocked the door and stepped into the sleeping interior. The place was strewn with dustsheets and spider webs, nothing offering invitation beside a damp, black fireplace.

Setting her bag down on the kitchen table, she looked about the place. It had been empty of any souls for a long time. Ahes was gone, and she knew without having to be told that Tomas had died. She was the only one left.

It would not be straight to bed on this first visit, for too much needed to be done. She would get the dustsheets taken down and chase out the spider webs. The main cleaning and washing could wait until tomorrow and daylight. Outside in the woodshed there were still some logs, and she quickly got a fire going in the hearth. A crackle of sparks and the deep glow of a wood fire brought a corner of warmth back to this forgotten cottage.

In the early morning sunlight started to filter through the grimy windowpanes. Isobella opened her eyes and gazed out over the room, watching the dust particles dance through beams of light. She would have to clean and organise the place before she could start working on brewing up fresh tincture for her bottles.

When she opened the door to go and fetch water from the well, she was greeted by a small black cat with white paws and a white tipped tail. The cat looked up at her as if to ask what excuse she had for trespassing. Isobella crouched down to meet the cat. This was not Tomas, but there was something quite familiar about the creature. She held out her hand, and the cat approached to sniff her knuckles before deciding that she was safe. The eyes narrowed in satisfaction and the creature took a quick stroll around the squatting human figure. "Tomasina," Isobella said quietly. "I shall call you Tomasina."

Isobella was industrious the first day, washing and sweeping the grime and dust from the cottage. Water and vinegar and a scrubbing motion got the filth from the windows, and sunlight burst into the kitchen. She sang loudly, old folk songs from the Breton coast that Ahes had sung to her whilst growing up. More wood was chopped and stacked in the woodshed. Curtains and sheets washed in the hot stove and hung out to dry. The furious ripping out of weeds to clear the paths around the cottage and through the garden was done in a flurry of eagerness. The more precise task of tending the garden would have to wait for a calmer moment. For now she wanted the cottage clean and lived in once again, a more settled space so that she could start her preparations.

Tomasina had wandered off into the woodland for most of the day, to hunt or sleep in some quiet corner. She returned in the evening, her hunger satisfied, to curl up on a cushion on the stool by the fire, now glowing and crackling as the autumnal night drew in.

For the rest of the week Isobella worked her garden, removing that which should not be there, and taming those plants which had taken advantage of the mistressless property. In the long bed of deadly nightshade, the plant reigned unchallenged. It had become overgrown and unruly, but as Isobella intended to make a lot of the tincture, she was happy to give the plant a hard prune. Armfuls of branches were laid out on the kitchen table. Isobella hurried between garden and kitchen with something of a breathless anticipation. She felt alive, more real than she had done in years.

The rains came and she filled buckets and pans with fresh rainwater. The fires were stoked and she worked long into the nights, boiling and straining off plant matter, reducing and refining the precious liquid. During a break in the rain, she left the kitchen and considered the pocketbook calendar from her bag. She counted off the days she had been in the cottage. She ought to be arriving back for work in London this morning. She watched the sunlight jig in raindrops caught on leaves. She would not return to that job. She would stay here. She felt an inner calmness, and close to her mother. She found one of Ahes' old pipes on the shelf by the door, along with a little stale tobacco. She tried to smoke it, remembering how peaceful Ahes had looked when she'd sat out in the garden with her pipe. The acrid smoke curled up in the back of her throat and tied her up in spasms of coughing. Each to their own. Smoking clearly wasn't for her.

The weeks passed by and Isobella sunk deeper into her isolated eccentricity. She batched up her prepared tincture, and on finding more bottles and vials in a cupboard, brewed extra so that she now had supplies to see her through years, if not decades.

Through six degrees of searching, London reached out to her in the form of Miss Rees one autumn morning. The leaves were an intense golden orange, and when the wind blew handfuls would flutter to the ground. Horse chestnuts lay cracked open in their silky shells. Miss Rees did not walk so well, and it had taken her some hours to get to the cottage. She had not seen Isobella since the first day she had arrived back in Wales. Miss Rees had assumed she had hurried back to London a long time ago. Yesterday a letter had arrived from Madame Maurier, who had heard from a Harriet Cunningham, nee Rothers, who had had it from an Italian by the name of Rosa, that Isobella had been lost for weeks, and had never returned to her job with the Ministry of Defence. No one knew if she had become lost or met with an unfortunate moment and an unmarked grave in the blitz upon her return to the capital. Perhaps she had suffered a mental breakdown, for she had seemed a little strange. Or maybe she had defected, the worst and silliest of rumours suggested. Nonsense, for the woman's allegiance on the continent was to France and the Brittany Coast. Madame fancied she had gone off to fight the resistance, for she could never see a happy settled home for Miss Donagh, filled with the usual comforts that most women longed for. But Madame wished to be certain, and as the last most definite fact was that Isobella had been travelling to Wales, she thought she would write and ask Miss Rees if she had seen the girl.

Isobella heard Miss Rees before she saw her. She nipped into the cottage and checked herself in the mirror. The effects had worn off and her pupils were back to their natural size. She still felt a little light headed, but that was all.

"Isobella Donagh!" Miss Rees exclaimed. She did not know whether to be angry or relived. "What are you doing still here?"

"Miss Rees," Isobella hurried out to greet her. She hugged the older woman eagerly. Tomasina hopped up onto the garden wall to survey the newcomer.

Miss Rees patted the girl's back, glad to find her well and alive. The warm feeling overrode the anger that the responsibilities of a job were not being taken seriously. She looked over at the little cat. "I see you've made a friend."

"This is Tomasina. Will you come in? I can make tea."

"Yes, I suppose I will." Miss Rees felt a little bemused, and if she was honest, apprehensive. There had always been an element of the odd about Isobella, and now that she was fully absorbed back into this isolated homestead, Miss Rees didn't know quite what she was going to discover. But it had been a long walk and her legs were aching. She needed a rest. She gingerly entered the cottage, and was pleasantly surprised by how clean and warm it was inside. "You've been busy."

"Getting things back to how they were." Isobella poured water into the kettle and hung it on the range. She got two teacups down from the dresser. "I'm sorry I didn't come to see you again. I've been caught up in cleaning out the cottage."

"I can see that. You've been missed in London."

There was silence, but for a chink as she set one of the teacups down in a saucer. "Oh."

Miss Rees sighed. "You ought to be more aware of your responsibilities. From what I've been told, you had a very good job with the Ministry. Good prospects."

"Been told?"

"Madame Maurier heard that you'd disappeared. People are worried. Some think you've been killed in one of these dreadful bombing raids I hear about on the wireless."

"Yes," she sat down and shook her head. "I mean no. I've been here. I've been cleaning."

"I can see," Miss Rees said kindly. "Is there a reason why you haven't been back? Is it the bombing that scares you?"

"No."

"Problems?"

"No."

"You're not feeling you have to hide away?" Miss Rees shuffled awkwardly. The subject of things that ought not to be spoken of, especially amongst unmarried women. "I mean, you're not in trouble, are you? The trouble."

Isobella creased her brow. She didn't know what Miss Rees meant, but shook her head regardless.

"Well, that's something."

Isobella fetched the tea caddy.

"When will you be going back? You ought to telegraph and let them know..."

"No."

"Or write."

"No." She lowered her eyes. Her head was feeling heavy all of a sudden. "I'm not going back."

"Not going back? What on earth will you do?"

"I want to stay here. I'll spend the winter here."

"In this little place?" Miss Rees looked around in horror. It was very cosy, but there was something out of kilter. And to think of a young woman all alone, utterly cut off in the cold shivers of winter. "I don't think that's such a clever idea. There's something... uncivilising about the place."

"I've not felt this well in a long time. Here is where I need to be."

In the end it was Miss Rees who wrote back to London to let the affected parties know that Isobella Donagh would not be returning. She was indeed in Wales and there was no need for concern. Miss Rees believed that the grief and sorrow of her mother's sudden demise had finally caught up with her. Isobella wasn't quite ready to come back into the world yet.

She did not see another human being that winter. There were times when she was quite certain she did, when the tincture took a hold of her senses and transported her to another plain of consciousness. The light broke apart into its separate colours. Isobella felt her heart race and her mouth grow dry in anticipation. Her eyes became ever widening pools of darkness. Gasping and grasping. The outline of objects split apart and multiplied, softly vibrating to create a blurred edge. Ahes sat on the garden wall smoking her pipe and laughing. Snow fell in deepest winter. Isobella ran naked through the trees under moonlight.

One night she was spinning in the kitchen garden. Tomasina had caught a mouse that turned into a fish as it was dropped onto the path. Isobella threw back her head and laughed, talking with the stars. It was a strange new language for not even she could understand a word she was saying. She took a vial of tincture from her pocket and dropped liquid into her already stretched eyes. Starlight rushed at her and she cavorted to the distant galaxies.

Somewhere in the dance she lost her balance. Perhaps a root had darted up to trip her. Time moved slowly as she waved her arms and fell over, collapsing into the deadly nightshade. The plants caught her, branches parting to allow her to sink to the ground. Leaves brushed her face on the descent. The foliage flicked back up around her, creating a warm nest where she could curl, in a foetus position, against mother earth. Isobella listened to the sound of her own breath as she stared up at the stars. It was cold and she breathed smoke. A small, tiny confused dragon found itself in the wrong time and place. Ice crystals gathered in her hair. She closed her eyes.

When she next opened her eyes full sunlight shone on her face. Isobella squinted, groaning at the shock of suddenly being awake. She struggled up. The leaves of the nightshade rustled irritably as she disturbed the peaceful sleep. Out on the garden path lay a dead mouse. Judging by the length of shadows it was around midday.

Grumbling, feeling hung over and unhelpful, she wandered back into the cottage. She shuddered, noticing that her fingers were tinged with blue. The fire had gone out.

"*Gast.*"

She grimaced. Her arms heavy, she grabbed at the fire bucket and slung firewood into the grating. Fumbling with matches and pieces of ripped up newspaper, she eventually got the fire going again, her eyes stinging with the damp smoke determined to blow back into her eyes. Coughing, Isobella tumbled back onto her rump. She sat for some time in front of the fire, warming her hands and hypnotically watching the flames grow.

Passing the mirror, she was a little shocked by her appearance. Her hair was tangled and bushed up. It looked like a bird's nest, complete with leaves and dry twigs. There were light streaks of mud on her pale face. She looked tired and drawn, like a corpse re-emerged from the grave.

There were precious few supplies in the cottage, and she hadn't seen another human being for weeks if not months. She would have to return to the village. Fetching a bucket of ice-chilled water from the well, she scrubbed herself down in front of the fire, gasping at the sharp bite of the water. Dirt and grime was sluiced from her flesh, her hair washed and brushed, and fresh clothes taken from the cupboard. She pulled winter boots onto her feet and slung one of Ahes' old workbags over her shoulder.

Leaving Tomasina curled up asleep by the fire, she set off into the woods in the direction of the village.

It was late afternoon when Isobella arrived. Village life was busy, although many kept indoors to avoid the chill. Conversations stopped and eyebrows were raised when people saw her approach. She had not been seen since that first day months ago. Many assumed she had gone back to the city. Other gossips said she was back out in that secret place in the forests where her mother had once communed with the devil. She had gradually been forgotten until Miss Rees went out walking into the woods. The rumour mill started up again temporarily. No one really understood why Miss Rees worried about that girl as much as she did. Isobella Donagh was not one of them. She had a strange look about her. Better off in London by far.

The more dramatic of the gossips had been right, and she had been somewhere in the forests all of this time. Isobella wandered past in an unconcerned manner, where others would have felt the stabbing eyes crawling up their spine. She went into the village store and bought what she needed, served by a silent woman who only opened her mouth to state the payment required.

Stepping back out into the street the wind picked up, whipping through her hair to begin the process of entanglement again. She pulled her scarves closer around her, and started in the direction of Miss Rees' cottage. Further up the little street a small cluster of women were muttering quietly amongst themselves. They became soundless as Isobella passed, only the expression on their faces changing. Eyes narrowed. No one ever spoke of these things, but for the women whose husbands had met Isobella, they knew how she could haunt their dreams.

"Witch."

She was at the top of the street, close to Miss Rees' cottage, when she heard the word. It was quietly spoken, but sharp and to the point. It had come from the group of women, but it sounded as if it had been spoken directly beside her ear. Her foot paused in the next step onwards. Isobella's social interaction with the wider world had never been particularly in tune, but even she realised that the word had been sent for her, and not in a kindly way. She did not look around. She continued to Miss Rees', knocking on the door. Solitude she could survive. But hate? Hate born of a strange kind of fear. She did not understand it. She had never harmed another woman.

There was no reply. Isobella cautiously opened the front door. She did not feel inclined to walk back past that group just yet. Inside she could smell the fire, hear the comforting crackle of the homestead. "Miss Rees?" she called out. "It's Isobella."

Miss Rees was in the winged armchair by the fire with a crocheted shawl across her knees. Her eyes were closed and her head bowed in thought. Isobella smiled and walked up to her, gently touching her hand as if to wake her. She quickly recoiled when she felt the waxen chill of the flesh. Crouching down, she took a better look at the woman, with her blue lips and still body. She was not breathing. In truth, she was not even there anymore. Just flesh and bones remained.

Isobella darted away and retreated to the wooden bench at the back of the room. What was it one did when someone died? She had never come upon a dead body before. Certainly she had helped some on their way, but that had been their desire. Not a natural passing. And what of Ahes? She had been killed in an accident and buried before Isobella had been told. She could still remember that day, when Miss Rees, Mr Griffiths the solicitor and PC Morgan had appeared in the forest. They had come to the cottage assuming it was no longer inhabited.

PC Morgan. The police dealt with this kind of thing. There was no mystery about it; Miss Rees had simply passed away from natural causes. But something ought to be done. The woman could not be left to rot in her chair. Isobella neither lived here nor was family. She was hardly in the rightful position to bury the woman out in the garden.

Hopping up, she hurried out of the cottage and into the village to locate the police officer. She ignored the stares and mutterings of women who did not dare to look her in the eye.

It was dark by the time it felt appropriate for Isobella to leave. She had done her duty by Miss Rees and the cottage was now empty. Miss Rees had left. Dour faced men had come to the cottage. Messages were sent, arrangements made and heads shook. People were polite but left her alone in the corner. After the coroner had spoken to her, it felt right to leave.

There were not many lights on in the village. Everyone tried to do their bit for the war effort, no matter how far flung they were, and blackout curtains were religiously drawn against night. Isobella had particularly keen eyesight and had no trouble in finding her way down the little roads. Only light from the pub spilled into the outer world from a partially open door. A couple of men were coming out, still full of the gossip of Miss Rees' passing and the odd circumstances of the discovery. Isobella Donagh, whom everyone had either hoped or presumed was in London, had appeared that afternoon pale and dark, like the grim reaper. She had been in the store briefly, then gone directly to Miss Rees. The next thing anyone knew, PC Morgan had been fetched and Miss Rees was officially dead. Common sense told people it had been a natural passing, but the gossip enjoys drama and Isobella's appearance, however coincidental could not be overlooked. The two men nodded to one another as they saw Isobella pass. One leaned back into the pub to say something to a friend. Isobella was probably just an eccentric hermit who was suffering psychologically from the upbringing Ahes had put her through. But some of the women used the word witch when they talked of her. No one could survive alone out in the woods that long. And weren't there old tales of a real witch who'd had a cottage deep in the forest a couple of hundred years ago?

Isobella never reacted so that anyone would have seen, but she heard the whispers and the footsteps as the group of men followed her at a distance out of the village. The heady stink of desire mixed with fear and violence made for a sickening perfume. She walked up green lanes, past fields, aware that she was being followed. Two thoughts occurred to her. She could not allow them to discover the location of the cottage. Certainly PC Morgan had been there, but she doubted he would be able to find it again without Miss Rees' guidance. Secondly she knew they intended to do something with her when they caught up with her. They hadn't decided exactly what, driven on by conflicting chemicals. One man she could have dealt with on her own, but five at once? As long as she could get into the forest before they caught up with her, all would be well.

Pulling her scarves tight to her body, Isobella picked up the pace and went into a quick march, head down against the chill. She could see the tree line. A couple of the men nudged one another, noting the increase in speed. She would be harder to catch in the forest. They had intended to drag her down into one of the green fields. Under the cover of darkness they would enact dreams, show her that one couldn't behave that way in a place like this. It wasn't right for a woman to be away so alone like that.

Comfort enveloped her as she stepped past the first tree and over the line from fields to forest. She heard the men break into a run. She hurried into the shadows, swiftly moving away from natural paths, into thorny undergrowth that parted before her intuition. Up away into the tree canopy and out of sight.

"It's darker than Satan's soul in here," one of the men grumbled as they crashed into the forest. Loud, thoughtless footsteps. Stumbling as a line into the environment.

"She can't have gotten far."

They moved forward, one man swearing as low hanging branches hidden by shadows thrashed at his face.

"Isobella Donagh, we're wanting a word with you."

"Say it in English, she might not understand."

"Oh, she speaks Welsh alright."

They spread out, the sound of their heavy breathing blotting out all other noises. They couldn't see her. Isobella, curled around the trunk up in the canopy, watched down between the branches.

"She's not here."

"We saw her come in. She can't be that far."

"I can't hear a thing."

"There's no one here."

"She's disappeared."

"My wife says she has powers..."

One of the men yelled in terror, stumbling backwards and falling on his arse. Sudden movement had startled him. He pointed out into the fields, where a small retreating creature disappeared from view.

"What's the matter with you?"

"It made me jump."

"It was a hare."

A silence settled between them. They'd all heard the old wives' tales of witches turning themselves into hares. Nonsense of witchcraft. None really believed it, but the darkness was a great fuel for the imagination, and encouraged by a drop of alcohol, it was difficult for the brain to be rational. The fallen man got back onto his feet and the men nodded to one another. They were never going to catch her. They left the forest.

Isobella waited a long time before descending from the tree. She wanted to be sure they were safe in their beds with no thoughts of coming back. When her feet met the forest ground, she hurried back through the undergrowth, eager for sight of the cottage. Sooner or later someone would find it. Perhaps one of the forest gangs. A lot of the men were gone to the war now. It was only the older ones, the returned wounded, and the few essentials exempted from the call up who remained. A lot of the forest workers had been replaced by women. Lumber Jills. They could stumble onto her sanctuary sooner or later, and when one person found her, the gossip would spread.

In essence, she did not belong here. The cottage was her childhood and a bubble of sanctuary, but the rest of the world was encroaching on that isolated spot. These were not her people, and she was not welcome. She would have to leave. Her people, she pondered, whilst sitting at the kitchen table with the map book Ahes had given her many years ago. Their primary language was Breton. They were from the Brittany coast, in France. That was the place where she belonged. But there was a war going on and France was occupied. She could not go home yet.

Patience, she told herself. She closed the book. This war would end, and when it did, she would be on a boat to the continent. In the meantime there were lots of places in the United Kingdom where she could bide her time. She would leave in the morning.

It was in Paris that Isobella first heard of *La Petit Mort*. Three young women were in the same compartment on the train, waiting for departure, and giggling about one of the girl's recent escapades. In their chatter they assumed Isobella was asleep. She was merely dozing. Her attention pricked when she heard the word death.

It was curious that so many feared death and were sombre and melancholic when the subject was brought up. Yet with these women, perhaps the same age as Isobella, it was spoken of with giggles and hushed glances. One of the girls wasn't sure quite what they were talking of, and the other two had to explain. It seemed the leader of the pack had enjoyed this event with her sweetheart last night. 'The Little Death'. Isobella pondered in silence, her face a mask to her thoughts. The girls made it sound as though it was a highly enjoyable thing. Ecstasy. She thought back to the men in the woods with Ahes. The men in the Blitz. They had worn expressions of intense joy. And then death. *La Petit Mort*. Of course this would be a French thing, perhaps even specifically Breton, what did she know? Either way, she was certain she had come home.

After departing from her village in Wales, Isobella had been unable to come to France immediately. The war was still ongoing and France was a battleground of destruction and occupation. No one was travelling there. Ignoring the warnings of high risk of bombing raids, she travelled to the south coast of England, and took up an office job in Dover to bolster funds for her eventual departure from Great Britain. Things were further delayed when solicitors contacted her to advise that she had been named as Miss Rees' sole beneficiary. Isobella was detached from a lot of social norms, but was not so out of touch to not realise how this would be viewed back in the village. She instructed the solicitors by letter to sell everything, and in turn had to wait for all sales to be arranged and funds to be transferred before she could leave. She had no intention of returning.

It was almost a year after the end of the war before she finally set foot on French soil. This was a country still bleeding from the occupation, the bombings and the allied invasion. Infrastructure was in a speedy state of repair. Some of the bombed out houses were habitable again. There were still many tumbled ruins that had once been considered home. Along the coast it was littered with defences. Cold concrete outlook posts that were not to be used again sat empty. The blood of so many lost lives was still fresh in the earth.

She initially travelled to Paris, and spent a few weeks living there. Her ear soon tuned to the speech of the Parisian and she quickly adapted her accent so that to many she sounded like a local. They would never have guessed that she had grown up isolated in the forests of Wales. Paris was a very different city to London, and for her, much easier to live in. But in her heart French was not her inner soul and the city was not her natural environment. She needed to be in Brittany.

Getting out of Paris was reasonably straight forward. Trains were not up and running nationwide as the modern traveller would have liked, but over a couple of days, between trains, rides in cars and by foot, she got herself into Brittany. She barely slept, unable to stop until she had reached the coast. She headed for Brest, a town that had been utterly destroyed by the war and bombing.

Isobella had been prepared for destruction, but also a joyful homecoming. It was not waiting for her. Brest had been virtually flattened. The locals, those who were still there, were destitute and homeless. Living in the ruins, trying to scrape together a home and a living from a hopeless ruin. There was money coming from Germany for reparations, but the process of finance to city to reconstruction and rejuvenation took time. Society was still very raw, and her happy outburst of Breton was greeted with French and suspicion. Some even spat in her direction. She only found out later that ties between pro-Breton movements and the Nazis had given the old language a bitter taste. The groups were originally intended to bolster the standing of the language and take joy in the Breton culture. The war had destroyed a lot of good intentions. It was a year after the war but it still felt like yesterday to many, and with the Breton National Party having collaborated with the enemy, few wanted anything to do with anyone who would take such unadulterated joy in the local culture. Isobella soon left the city and took to camping out in the wilds along the coast. It was through rural folk, other tramps and those who would whisper Breton, ashamed that their beautiful language had been warped by such negative association, that Isobella learned how the language had essentially stabbed itself in the back and was dying out again. It was not the homecoming she had hoped for.

Isobella was well versed in the art of self sufficiency, and by the coast she was able to scavenge enough food to keep herself well fed. She found an old discarded curtain in a ruin that she waterproofed, and along with some timbers and rope, created herself a little tent. She erected it by the coast, up on cliff tops and hidden from most views by undergrowth. From the entrance to her tent she had a view out to the sea and the inky black of night when the sun dropped below the horizon. She dug a small fire pit, surrounded with sea bashed rounded stones, and fashioned a spit over which she could hang an old kettle and small soup kettle she had purchased from one of the villages. Many who were still here were destitute and would sell anything they could spare, and much which they shouldn't.

It was a simple case of avoiding the fact that her hopes had failed. She had no idea what to do next. She would forage in the wilds and the shore where it was safe to go into the water (there was still much refuse, barbed wire, mines and other deadly paraphernalia from the war). On an evening she would light the fire and watch the dusk descend. She would cook her food and sing old Breton songs that Ahes had taught her. Sometimes she would take a drop or two of her precious tincture and lay back in the soft grass and watch as the stars sparkled into life and began a heavenly ballet just for her.

On one such evening she had her first contact with the real true Breton. She was sitting on the grass by the fire, poking a spoon into her stew and singing a sea song in Breton. She knew she was being watched long before either acknowledged the other. She was safe in the knowledge she had her knife upon her person, and was bold in the naïveté of the inexperienced who have never been overpowered.

As the song came to an end, the stranger stepped out from the shadows of the trees, making the first sound as he snapped a twig underfoot. It could equally have been the natural end of the song or the intensifying scent of food that settled his mind to make contact. Isobella looked up to see a thin, gaunt man with dark sunken eyes, in ragged clothes loitering on the edge of her campsite. His hair was shaggy, the worst of the starvation in his face hidden by his prematurely greying beard.

"Pardon, Madame, I hope I have not startled you."

He spoke in Breton. Isobella smiled. Finally someone who would speak her language. "I knew you were there for some time." She gestured at the fire. "Will you join me? I've made quite a lot."

A starving man needs no second invitation. He was soon by the fire, folding his splintered limbs to take his place at her table. The reflected glow from the fire put some life back in his flesh. Isobella rustled through a cloth sack that held her ad hoc camping gear. She took out a pot generally used during foraging and offered it to him. "It's not really for eating out of, but I don't have many utensils. Not really fine dining..."

"Madame," he interrupted, gratefully accepting the vessel. "This looks like the most civilised dining I have seen in my life."

She smiled, lowered her eyes as she spooned out the stew. "Madame," she repeated. "No one calls me that. I am Isobella Donagh."

"Donagh?" he sounded surprised. "I thought you were Breton. Certainly you sound it."

"I am, although I've only arrived. My father was Irish. I never met him. My mother, she was from this part of the world."

"Ah," he nodded. Slurping some of the stew, for there was no cutlery to use, he then introduced himself. "I am Youenn," he said. "These days I am reduced to no more than you see before you, this shadow of a man."

"And you are Breton?"

"Of course. But even that is perhaps not something to boast of just now." There was a minute or two of silence in the conversation whilst they ate. "It is good to hear the old language again. Those songs. Your mother taught you?"

She nodded. "This is the first time I have been in Brittany. Unfortunately my mother passed away some years ago so I have come alone. It seems this part suffered heavily from the war."

"Indeed it has."

"I didn't realise..." she started. "Rather, I don't suppose I understand anything that has happened here."

He looked up at her from his bowl.

"People were angry when I spoke Breton. It's as if people don't want to admit to it."

He put his bowl aside. "This is the legacy of the war. It has destroyed so much more than we can understand. Believe me; your Breton brothers are not evil. Some were led astray or took the wrong path. Negativity rather than rejoicing of what we have and are. They thought the Nazi's would give them back Brittany and independence and purity." He looked bitterly out towards the dark sea. "That was not what *Seiz Breur* was supposed to be about."

"Seven brothers? You come from a big family?" Isobella didn't quite follow.

He smiled sadly. "You never heard the story of *Seiz Breur*? Did your mother not tell you?"

"No, I don't recall."

He put his bowl to the side. "Very well. A payment for the very fine meal you have provided. I can offer a story. It's an old folk tale."

Isobella settled into her shawls. Youenn lay back in the grass to begin the story. "There was a poor family. A man and a wife and seven boys. They were so poor, it was impossible for them all to live. So they said to these seven boys, that they must set out and seek their fortune. It would be better for them all, and this way they could find good lives.

"The mother was very saddened over this decision, but knew it was for the best as she waved goodbye to her children. Later she had another child, a girl, who grew up into a fine young woman. Once day a neighbour mentions these brothers to her, and the girl runs straight home to mother. She never knew she had any siblings. Her mother admits the truth to her. The girl decides she must go and find these seven brothers. She asks for enough linen to make seven shirts, and away she goes.

"She travels much and asks in many places where her brothers are. Eventually she finds out where they are living. When she arrives at the house they are out at work. But the house is in chaos. Ah, seven men in a house, you can imagine. So she begins to tidy up and when she hears they are returning, she goes and hides herself in a hole. They are very surprised to find someone has been cleaning. Every time they go she cleans some more. Then at night whilst they are sleeping she sits and sews the shirts, one for each brother each night. She leaves it on the bed whilst they are sleeping.

"It is on the seventh night, when she is laying the seventh shirt out, that her youngest brother wakes, and he realises that this is their sister. They are all very happy to be reunited.

"So she stays with her brothers, but they warn her that she must never go to the neighbour's farm. Of course one day she forgets and goes there, and there is a witch..."

"A witch? I think I've heard a story with a witch and seven men."

"Perhaps not quite this one. As I say, there was a witch at this farm. She gave the girl a parcel of herbs, and said they were very good for a footbath when one was tired. So that evening the girl prepared a footbath for her brothers when they returned from a long day of work. But of course this was an enchantment and the brothers were transformed into cows. They were all different cows. The youngest had been turned into a fine little Breton cow.

"Every day she took these cows out to the pasture, and she stood watching over them. One day the young king was riding by and he saw this beautiful young woman. From that moment he could have no other. It did not matter that she was so poor. True love." He sighed to himself and grew silent for a few moments as if remembering a happier time in his own life.

"Did he break the spell?"

"Eh? Oh no. The girl agreed to marry him, but she told him that he must never harm these seven cows, and especially not the little Breton cow. So they went to the king's castle and lived there in peace. But the witch heard of this fortune and was greatly vexed. She got into the castle and stole away with the girl and threw her into a precipice. She then returns to the castle and hops into the girl's bed to take her place. When the king returns he finds her changed, but cannot understand it. Because of course the witch has cast a spell. She tells the king that he must go out and kill those cows. She was a wicked witch, you understand.

"The king was perplexed, for his bride had always been so caring of these cows. And now she demanded their deaths. He went out to see the cows for himself. They were all stood at a precipice mooing. It was very strange. He went to the precipice to see what was bothering the beasts, and there he heard the voice of his beloved. He threw down a rope and she climbed up and told him of the witch. So they returned to the castle and dragged the witch out. He demanded that she break the spell over the seven brothers or she would be executed forth with. The witch complied and the brothers were free. Life was good and justice done."

"And the witch went free?"

"Oh no, they threw her into a piping hot oven anyway. It is the only thing to do with witches."

Isobella pursed her lips and folded her hands on top of one another. She had been called a witch, although she had certainly never cast an enchantment on anyone. She did not know how to do such a thing. Ought she to be thrown in an oven?

"That is where our name came from," he continued. "Although Seiz Breur today is our artistic union, or at least it was. It was supposed to be a celebration of Breton, of our art and our skills." He sat up again, enlivened by the ideology. "We were writers, artists, craftsmen, musicians. It was good. It was true. But then some believed we needed to purify the Breton, to gain independence from France and they thought the Nazis could be their saviours. I did not follow that. But I am tarnished with the same brush. And many cannot bear to hear Breton. It has all gone terribly wrong."

He put his hand up to brush his tangled hair back off his forehead. Isobella noticed for the first time that his right hand was damaged. There were healed wounds and scars of cuts and terrible burns. Three of the fingers seemed to be fixed in the one curled position like a claw.

"What do you do? Are you a writer?"

He looked sadly at her. "I am nothing," he said quietly. "Before the war I was a carpenter. I carved wood. Now those pieces I created have burned and all I have is..." he held up his damaged hand in front of his face. "I could not even make them again. There are still members who can still practice their art, and they still use the Breton. But this is still a fresh wound, you understand. The war has not long since finished. Very horrific things happened. Some will continue, others are gone forever. I am merely a shadow now." He paused. "Madame, I am not a danger. Would it be acceptable to you if I stayed by your fire this night and slept? I feel as though this has brought a little comfort to my bones."

"Of course. It has been good to be able to hear and speak my mother tongue with someone."

"*Trugarez*," he gave thanks as he lay back into the grass and closed his eyes.

Isobella nodded and shuffled back into her little tent. *"Netra,"* she assured him. *"Netra."*

Youenn spent the next couple of days with Isobella. They talked and foraged for food. Many hours were spent sitting, Isobella listening to the history of her people. More songs and more legends were committed to memory.

Perhaps it had been the good company or the temporary nuclear feeling of a family that the two brought together suddenly, but on the second day he broke down and the facts of his own past came forth. He was distraught. He did not want to live anymore, he told her. He had been a father of two little girls who had been killed during a bombing raid. Crushed in their collapsed family home. His wife had become a mute shadow after that terrible day, and a few months afterwards had committed suicide. He had been alone ever since, living like a tramp, haunted by their memory and the crumbling of his own culture and language. Two pleasant days of company had brought everything back. Life could be good, but for him there was no hope. He could no longer go on.

Isobella had eyed her bag as he had told her these stories. She had thought of the vials of tincture therein. She could bring about his most earnest wish and take him to death. It was true that this was what people, men especially longed for. She made a decision that she would do it the following day, but when she woke the next morning Youenn had departed without leaving any kind of message. She supposed he had gone somewhere to complete the deed himself.

She spent the next few days following the same routine, and then it was the full moon. She went down to the cove where she knew it was safe from mines, barbed wire and other defensive remains of the war. Adding a drop of tincture to each eye, she felt her awareness expand. Her eyes gasped open to the starlight as she leant back to stare up at the heavens. She waded out into the sea, thigh deep, and held open her arms. Celestial bodies danced and sprinted down towards her. It was beautiful.

Unexpectedly Youenn returned that night as she was singing in the sea. He walked out into the tidal salt water and joined her. He smelt strongly of alcohol, and had he been sober he would have realised that something was very wrong when she turned to look at him. Her hair was loose and blowing around her face, her eyes were two abnormally large black holes. She looked like a supernatural creature born of the waves. He was too intoxicated to understand.

He walked up to her and crushed himself upon her, kissing her hard in a loveless, desperate way. Isobella understood what he was asking of her, and she took him that night. In the morning, as she was disassembling her camp and packing her sparse belongings, Youenn's lifeless body bobbed face down in the waves. Finally at peace.

Isobella lost track of the weeks and months as she travelled the length and breadth of Brittany by foot. As the seasons rolled on she watched as communities gradually rebuilt themselves. The mental scars remained, but life began to wake up again and the mourning for the war melted away. Life was reborn and the opportunity could not be missed. Isobella tried to find Ahes' original village, hoping she would discover that corner where she belonged. She felt a common understanding with the people, and took joy when someone would speak Breton with her. But she was always the stranger just passing through, watching as locals started life again after the war. She never belonged; she never had a place to stay. In time it began to feel hopeless, a bittersweet homecoming. This was her native land, but in not growing up here, she had been unable to claim a stake. No one would miss her if she left.

In Lamballe she was sold a bicycle. Suddenly the miles could disappear beneath her with astonishing speed, and the extent of her range mushroomed. Perhaps her home was in France as an entirety and in obsessing over the Breton land, she had grown blind to her true home. She left Brittany to cycle throughout France, taking occasional office jobs here and there to supplement her funds and pay for accommodation. Living under the open stars in the countryside was blissful, but in towns it was necessary to conform to bricks and mortar. And so it went, the months drifting into years. Isobella lost track of the fact that she had ever had an ultimate goal in the first place.

A salty breeze, heated by the strength of summer and already hot by June, brushed over the seafront. White-topped waves lapped against the rocky outcrops. Even at the edge of land brightly painted buildings clustered as far out as architecture would allow. Boom time and beauty, and the sprawling seaport expanded in and out. Multi-storey houses crowded adjacent and almost on top of one another, threatening to tumble domino-like into the Mediterranean. The breeze picked up again and rustled through the expansive skirts of the red and white polka dot dress. Isobella, idly propped against a concrete post by the sea front, looked out onto the small sandy beach that dipped down into the blue waters of the sea. A few sunbathers were already out on their towels. Even from this distance she could hear their American voices chattering eagerly, as positive as the sun's rays. These young things were rich and free, off on their modern day Grand Tour before returning to the family arms to become leaders of industry or good model wives and matriarchs.

It was another world utterly alien to her, but one which she had heard much about from her flatmates. She had shared a pokey small flat with two female American students. The girls were art historians, or so they said, but had spent little time on their traditional studies, and much more on merry making and travel, mostly with compatriots. They had been mildly curious about Isobella's exotic background, but had never really gotten to the bottom of who she was, even after six months of cohabitation. Any curiosity they had was swiftly trampled down by chatter about themselves. The two girls had departed last week, having taken their fill of Genoa and eager to see something new. They had a three month rental at Naples, and then it would be to Roma for the autumn.

The apartment had been in chaos when they'd left. The clutter they had arrived with: cases and cases of clothes, shoes and jewellery, record players, books, pictures and engravings, had mushroomed over a six month stay. Each girl had been forced to purchase an additional case before leaving Genoa. Some things had been shipped home, others had to be abandoned. Isobella had inherited the halter neck dress with sprawling skirts that she now wore. She also had an empty flat of three bedrooms that she couldn't afford on her office salary. She'd left a notice at the American Express office and was sure she would fill the space soon. She was not worried.

A cluster of five Italian girls, all wearing bright red lipstick and chattering loudly and gaily, for summer was coming, passed by Isobella. A couple of Italian men clinging onto a scooter flew by, beeping their horn and waving their hands in exhilaration of so many pretty girls all at once. The sudden noise brought some more young men out of a cafe across the road, and the shouts of 'Ciao Bella!' started. It had taken Isobella some time to get used to the constant invasion of personal space many an Italian man thought appropriate to a woman of a certain age. Although she spoke Italian when she arrived in the country, she had been confused at first as to how so many knew her name. Every day they would call out to Bella Donna. The two words simply meant beautiful woman of course, but sounded so close to her own name, Isobella Donagh, that she would wonder if she had a stray name tag hanging off her bag. Either that or somehow news of her arrival had preceded her, although she couldn't think why anyone would have been interested.

The group of young women clearly had a destination in mind, and brushed off the men with sharp words. Attention shifted to Isobella. She was not ideal prey, as a single woman and not enough for all the men of the group – certainly not for one each. But a single woman was an easier catch and they had quickly sauntered across the road. With her dark hair and her skin that baked to olive under the sun, Isobella easily passed for an Italian. It was only when she spoke more than a few words, that an accent became apparent on certain sounds. It was almost French. And so the Ciao Bellas started up again. It was an appreciation of youth's fine looks as if she was just a statue to be admired and talked about. As if she were either deaf or too stupid to comprehend anything more than simplistic compliments.

A motorised roar accompanied a little Vespa scooter that pulled up to the group. Its driver was a bearded young man of academic look with no helmet, for these were days long before health and safety. Isobella politely smiled and slipped through the gaggle of men as the Vespa approached. She hopped onto the seat behind the driver and slipped her arms around his waist. The voluminous skirts of her dress flounced up around her legs. There was a moment of pantomime of tragedy that she was leaving the hormone pumping young stallions. The Vespa started to move again and roving eyes swiftly trawled for the next pretty face.

The Vespa weaved its way through the narrow twisting streets of Genoa, away from the sea. The engine worked harder as the land began to incline upwards. The intense mesh of buildings began to thin out, and the couple climbed out of the city fug into the forested hills that peaked above the maritime city. The sun baked the rocky dry earth. The trees provided some shade for creatures thoughtless enough to be out in the midday sun. A light breeze shifted through the leaves.

They stopped off at a small *ristorante*, spending a couple of hours eating, drinking and taking in the atmosphere before continuing to rise in altitude. The bike followed narrow country lanes, ever further away from habitation until it felt as though they were the only two people left. The young man parked the Vespa in the shade of trees off the side of the road. He took his satchel off the bike, adding a paper and a bottle of wine to the contents. They stepped into the woodland. Dry crackling twigs snapped underfoot as they entered the undergrowth.

This tract of land had become Isobella's sanctuary when she had moved to Genoa almost a year ago. She spent much of her free time here, long before she met Alberto and his Vespa, and had built up a reasonably detailed mental map of the lie of the land. She was by far the most familiar with the forests and yet when accompanied by the young man, he always chose to lead the way and find a place where they would sit and talk. Isobella didn't usually give it a second thought as she was here enough on her own at other times to do as she wished.

A site was eventually selected, in a small glade where the trees broke apart. Dry, sun-warmed grass made a comfortable place to sit. The wine was opened and passed between the couple.

Isobella lay back and gazed up at the sky. It was a bright blue framed by vivid green fluttering leaves. Alberto sat and read the paper. The crinkling sound as he turned a page blended with the noise of a breeze through the forest foliage.

"You know, when I read things like this, I sometimes think about changing my direction."

There had been silence for some time and Isobella had been starting to doze off. She opened her eyes.

"I always thought my ultimate goal was surgery, but sometimes when I read these stories I do wonder about psychiatry." Alberto was a student of medicine. He was a rather serious and studious young man, confident in his intellectual abilities and keen to unravel puzzles wherever he found them. He tapped at the article he had been reading. "There's been another man murdered. His body was found at the *Staglieno Cimitero*."

"It's a fitting place for a body," Isobella mused.

He smiled lightly. "When the body is officially interred, yes. But this man was found behind the Pantheon building, just discarded. His throat was slit. One single, deep practised cut. To try and understand the mind that did this. Perhaps even to rehabilitate..."

"These are just the acts of criminals, gangs..."

"Ah, no," Alberto sounded pleased that she was falling into the same trap as so many others. "This is not a criminal execution of any kind. These types of murders have been happening in the north of Italy for the last couple of years."

"Italy is full of criminals."

"I tell you, it's not the gangsters you imagine. These bodies, these men were in the throes of passion and then they were murdered. I have seen particular cases reported in the news, and I can distinguish them from the usual criminal executions. Believe me, there is a serial killer creeping around the north."

Outwardly Isobella made no sign, but internally her attention picked up. "So you think their lovers are killing them?"

He smiled kindly. "Bella, Bella. Believe me, this is not the work of a woman. It is a man. Perhaps he is impotent. Perhaps it is a type of woman he stalks, and when he finds her with another man..." He left the thought unspoken. "But it is always in a remote place, or a quiet time, and outdoors. Two lovers have gone away to be together, and they think they are alone. But there is someone watching."

Isobella propped herself up on her elbows. "So are we in danger now? Out here in the woods."

"I will look after you. Besides, we are just talking. It does not fit with the pattern."

"No, of course not. We are just talking." Isobella sighed as she flopped back down into the grass.

Alberto lowered the paper and looked over at her, having caught the tone in her voice. Although he assumed they were of the same age, there was something contradictorily ageless and ancient about Isobella. Subconsciously it made him feel a little out of his depth. She was not exactly the most talkative woman he had ever been with, and could be hard to read at times. An enigma, perhaps something to study if he did shift his career direction from the surgical to the mind.

They had been seeing one another for around two months now, and he had still not found quite the opportunity to make love to her yet, his confidence often strangely faltering. In previous dalliances, not only would the deed have been committed long before, but also the connection long broken off. He was a young man with his life ahead of him, and most girls, fresh from the country and moving to the cities in search of work in the industrial boom, did not have much to keep his attention. Isobella was quite singular. Maybe it was because she was foreign.

Perhaps emboldened by the wine, thinking his time was now, he moved across to her. He picked up her hand and kissed the inside of her wrist. "You are a very beautiful woman," he told her. "I don't think I've ever been with such a beauty. I would love to see your whole beauty."

A few minutes later Isobella thought to herself how odd it was to be with a man and yet to have not taken her tincture. It was an odd experience. Now the only thing she wore was the necklace with the small crystal vial pendant. It was slippery with sweat. Alberto had insisted on being on top, and was plugging away. She felt rather passive. His breathing was heavy, become faster and faster. The moment of *la petit mort* was approaching and she knew what she would have to do for him regardless that she had not moved up to her higher level of awareness. She reached out for her crumpled dress to pull out the pocketknife.

Alberto's eyes fluttered open momentarily as a flash of sunlight slithered over the knife. A panic switched on in his brain, and he lurched backwards at the moment of coming, just out of reach from Isobella's sweeping arch.

He left her abruptly, his body spent as he staggered back onto his feet. "What are you doing?" he yelled at her. "Do you think that is funny, after what I was just telling you?"

"But that is what you want."

"What I want?" he gasped, unable to comprehend how she could be quite this stupid. Isobella wasn't like the dumb country girls he'd had. He watched as she sat up, the sunlight washing down her smooth flesh. This was too sharp a contradiction. "You could have cut me."

"You wanted to die."

"What are you talking about, you little fool? I am young; I have my whole life ahead of me. I was enjoying the body of a..."

"But this is what all men want."

"All men…"

"*La petit mort.*"

Alberto snorted. "That is just a French expression. It's not meant to be taken literally. It's just the orgasm." He happened to glance down at his flaccid member and felt ridiculous. He pulled on his trousers. As he was shrugging his arms into his shirt, he watched Isobella, calmly looking at her little knife.

"All men want this?" he said. "Please don't tell me you had something to do with that man at the cemetery."

"He looked so happy."

Alberto drew the air sharply in between his teeth. He crouched down a few metres from her. "Bella, no one wants to die, and certainly not like that. You are deluding yourself. You are deluded."

She did not know what to say. This was a sobering revelation. Not all men wanted to die? Not at that moment of enjoyment? Had she misunderstood the human condition all this time? Had Ahes been wrong? What of those lost young men buried out in the Welsh forests? And all the others? But there had been those who wanted to die. The carpenter in Breton had not wished to continue. He had to die. There were those who should. Things had suddenly grown very complicated. She was too hot to think.

Perhaps from a touch of shock, Alberto had sat down again and folded himself up in thought. He still could quite not believe that Isobella could have committed such acts. How could such a beauty do these things? She must have some mental condition that confused her thinking. But it was not lost. He had seen already from talking to her that she was confused. She could be saved. "I can help you."

Isobella looked up sharply. What did that mean? Take her to the authorities? To say that she was not a saviour, but just a killer. A killer that had a witness. The state of her situation changed drastically. She knew what the authorities liked to do to murderers.

He was sitting side on to her, paying no attention. He stared at his hands. "I can solve this. I know what is best for you."

"No." She scrambled forward. It was trying enough to live in civilisation at times. She only survived because she could flee back into nature when the world grew too stifling. But to be locked into a concrete cell, that would kill her. She would die.

With one neat slash it was over, the deep rend burning crimson. He wore a look of surprise as he continued to stare down at his hands, watching the deep vermillion blood pour down the front of his body, over his fingers and into the earth.

Isobella quickly dressed, careful to stay outside of the blood splatter so as not to soil her dress. Brushing the dust down from herself, she left the scene and moved deeper into the forest. She didn't return to the Vespa, and instead crossed over, meeting a usual route she took when she came here alone. Passing by an old ruined fort, now soldiered with sapling trees, she started her descent back into Genoa.

Dusk had bedded the city down for the night by the time Isobella returned to her apartment. As she walked in off the street she felt numbed and bewildered. Although the imminent problem had been dealt with, she had been left with many questions.

She started the ascent to her apartment on the third floor. As she turned the final corner to reach her home, a door on the floor below opened and a voice called up to her.

"Isobella?"

She paused and looked back down the staircase.

100

"I thought it might be you." The American girl, Zoey or Joey or something, she could never quite remember, bounded up towards her. There were quite a few rich Americans staying in the building. They only lived here for a month or two, before heading off to the more culturally popular cities of Rome, Florence, Pisa, Naples... and onwards towards Greece. They had no responsibilities, only a couple of years of freedom paid for by ma and pa. Crates of souvenirs shipped back home and most of what they'd seen and learned forgotten. Once one had found a flat, news got around, and others moved into the building, finding some comfort in being surrounded by their countrymen. In some ways it lessened the native experience for the travellers, but for Isobella it did provide a ready and constant stream of newcomers to share the rent.

"Listen," the girl said, "You've not found any new girls yet to share the flat, have you?"

"No, it's only early days."

"Fantastic. I was down at American Express this morning collecting my mail and I got talking to these two sisters from New York. They just arrived this morning. They're absolute dolls; you're going to love them. They want to stay in Genoa six weeks, can't afford a hotel for that amount of time, and I told them, your luck's in, girls. There's two rooms in an apartment above mine that have just been vacated. Great location, and third floor means fantastic views..."

Isobella was exhausted by the torrent of chatter. She needed to go lie down in a dark room. "Of course. Tell them to call by sometime."

"Well, they're right downstairs in my apartment. Why don't they come up and take a look now?" Without waiting for a reply Zoey scurried back down the sweeping staircase to her new friends.

Isobella inwardly sighed. She didn't want to talk to anyone just now, but she did need new flatmates as soon as possible. She might as well get this over with.

Zoey's eager voice echoed back up the stairs before the girls arrived. "Honestly, you're just going to love this place. I wish I'd moved in, but it was already full when I got to Genoa so I had to take a place on the second floor. And the other girl, Isobella, she's just a doll."

There was a murmured question as one of the girls came out of Zoey's apartment.

"What? Oh no, she's not a local either. She's French, but her English is so good. Really, you could almost believe she's a native."

The Americans appeared. The sisters were dressed in complimentary coloured silk dresses, white gloves up to their elbows and matching hats. For a moment Isobella wondered if they were twins, but on closer inspection she guessed that the girl in the green dress was the elder by a couple of years.

"This is Eleanor Harrington," Zoey introduced the eldest girl first. "And her sister Rosemary. Just arrived in Genoa this morning. Girls, this is Isobella Donagh."

"Donagh?" Rosemary gasped, looking a little confused.

"*Isobella* Donna?" Eleanor repeated, putting the Italian stress onto the words. "Did you adapt your name for the country, or is that just an uncanny coincidence?"

"It's Donagh, Irish," Isobella replied. "And the sounds are coincidence."

"Irish?" Zoey lowered her brows. "I thought you were French. You're Irish?"

"No. My father was, but I have never been to Ireland."

Zoey's facial features relaxed. "Ah, ok, I see the connection. But French born and bred. That'll be why you speak such good English. Well, come on, girls; let's take a look at the apartment."

Zoey, an estate agent in the making took charge and led the sisters through the flat, explaining the various features of Italian living and what they could expect from the apartment. And of course Isobella would be happy with six weeks, and of course they could pay on a weekly basis. Isobella loitered in the small shared living room and waited for the tour to be completed. The sisters seemed happy with the prospect and Eleanor asked when they would be able to move in. Whenever they could start paying rent, Isobella replied.

It was agreed they would move in the next day. They were eager to get closer to real Italian life and away from the sterile tourist experience. They were travelling to learn, and the sisters wanted to use this opportunity to improve their spoken Italian. Zoey had burst out that Isobella was fluent and would be able to teach them. Isobella had politely declined, explaining that she also worked full time. Besides, she had a French lilt to her Italian, and they would want to learn from a native in order to try and mimic the accent better.

When the girls had gone, Isobella locked the door and went to bed. She opened her bedroom windows wide and lay on her bed, gazing at the dark ceiling and trying to order her thoughts. Not all men wanted to die. In fact, most of them wanted to live on. If this was the truth, then what had been happening all these years? What had she done? She wondered if she ought to feel remorse, but she only felt cold and silent. She had never seen any distress or regret. There had never been a chance. They were often caught up in that intense moment, unable to think beyond those seconds, and suddenly it was all over. There were no screams, no desperate pleas for life. She remembered the scenes from the woodland when Ahes had been at work. It was just the same.

She rolled onto her side in bed and looked out at the building across the narrow street. She could hear a man shouting at his wife. Soon there would be the sound of slaps and sobbing. Perhaps one of the children would wake up and cry. If one could not assume that a man wanted to die, then what justification was there? Perhaps she ought to choose those who deserved to die. Take the man across the road for instance, who hit his wife most nights. It would certainly bring that woman some peace to be without that bully in her life. But who was Isobella to judge who had the right to live and die? Her hand stretched out to her bedside table, fingers brushing against an unopened vial. There was no reason. It was all random chance. Coincidence. Things just happened.

Isobella was out at work when the suitcases were deposited at the flat and the sisters spent the first day moving in. There was a lot of luggage, and a lack of storage space to hold the empty cases. They ended up creating a couple of extra side "tables" in the living room – basically piles of suitcases with pretty tablecloths thrown over the top. Isobella wondered if they were at the end of their tour and had a lot of souvenirs with them, hence the amount of luggage. Rosemary had laughed. Oh no, they'd only spent a month in Paris, that was all. They were going to 'do' Italy and Greece, then return to France next year to spend time touring when Eleanor's fiancé came over from the States.

The flat was suddenly full of noise, clutter and activity. On evenings Isobella would have a few hours of peace as the girls liked to go out and eat at restaurants, hang out in cafes or go to the opera or theatre. It was unsettling but she knew she would soon grow accustomed to the routine, and besides, this would only be for six weeks.

It was at the end of that first week when her assumptions were shattered.

The day before the sisters had mentioned that they were going to a cafe to see a jazz band that Friday evening, and Isobella had to join them. As there was no work the following day, she had agreed. It was as they were getting ready that things changed. A hammering of footsteps, then the door was wrenched open without waiting for invitation, and Zoey burst into the flat.

"Isobella," she cried out, "you poor thing. I just saw the police release."

She was standing at a mirror brushing her hair. The brush stopped mid stroke and she peered curiously in at her own reflection. Why was she worthy of pity?

Zoey was hovering in the bedroom door. She read Isobella's expression, then a look of horror poured over her own face. "Oh my goodness, you don't know, do you?"

She put the brush down. "Know what?"

Zoey had a newspaper in her hand. She glanced down at it, looking guilty. "Oh, I don't know if I should be the one breaking it to you. It's simply awful."

"Breaking what?"

"It's just dreadful. My Italian isn't fantastic, so I don't follow it all, but I know enough to get the basics."

"Just what on earth has been happening?" Eleanor appeared in the hallway behind Zoey. "All this shouting. We're getting ready to go out to the club. Aren't you coming, Zoey?"

"Well, yes, of course. It's just Alberto."

Eleanor smiled. "Alberto? I don't think I've met him. Is he a new beau of yours?"

Her eyes widened open. "No, he's Isobella's."

"Well, he can come too. I'm sure the place will hold another body."

Inwardly the realisation came to Isobella what this was all about. Her mind flashed back to the afternoon. She'd not given it another thought since she'd walked away. In fact, she had been too thoughtless. She was getting dressed again, keeping herself at a distance whilst she pulled on her dress to avoid getting any blood on it. Alberto lay in the grass, the last bubbles of life expiring from the gaping slice in his throat. The thick dark blood was spreading down the incline, soaking into the dry earth. Nourishing the surrounding plants. Isobella put on her shoes and walked away from the scene. Let alone a burial, she'd not even made an attempt to cover the body. The Vespa had been left at the side of the road.

Zoey had held up the newspaper for Eleanor to see. The girl put a hand to her mouth in horror. "Oh how ghastly."

They both turned to Isobella. "This is Alberto isn't it? I mean, your Alberto?"

Isobella took the newspaper. There was a drawing of Alberto, taken from his corpse and adjusted to remove the expression of horror and the slashed throat. It was unmistakably him. Her eyes scrolled through the information in the paper. The Vespa found up in the hills. His body discovered yesterday in the scrub and forest. Police believed it had been lying there for several days. His throat had been slashed. They did not believe it had been a robbery for no money had been taken. Comparisons were already been drawn with the body that had been discovered with its throat slit at the cemetery. The police were looking back into that case. They thought there was a mad man in Genoa. For public safety they were going to hunt him and lock him away.

Zoey touched Isobella's arm. "Are you alright?"

Lock him away.

"It'll be the shock," Eleanor said.

Lock him away.

"You've not heard from Alberto for a while?"

Lock her away.

Isobella shook her head slowly. "No, not for several days, but that's not unusual. I..." she faltered. There were things she ought to be saying to these girls. Plans she ought to be making in silence. But she couldn't trust herself to separate the silent and the vocal thoughts correctly. She could barely think. She'd never left herself exposed like this, never really considered the consequence of her actions. The thought of a cell terrified her. To not be able to stay under the stars. No more forests. No more tincture, no more trips. Her knees weakened and she bowed down as if about to collapse.

"Rosemary, get a glass of water," Eleanor yelled back into the flat.

The two girls helped Isobella to sit on the edge of the bed. She couldn't look at them. "This has been a terrible shock," she murmured.

"You bet it has," Zoey said.

Eleanor had taken the paper and was reading through the police notice. Her Italian was clearly far more advanced than Zoey's. "How dreadful. It says he was found up in the hills. His Vespa was found up there as well. As if he'd been lured."

"How was he when you last saw him?" Zoey blurted out.

"Zoey!" Eleanor gave her a sharp look.

"He was fine," Isobella whispered. He had been falling into peace when she had left.

"You might have been the last person to see him," Zoey added. "You went for a ride with him at the weekend."

How did she know that? Isobella didn't ever idly discuss her plans and she was sure she hadn't told Zoey. She must have seen her at the sea front when Alberto had picked her up. "I should go and speak to the police. Maybe they can tell me something."

"Do you want us to go with you?" Zoey asked, although she didn't sound keen. "I don't think I'll be much help, I don't speak Italian all that well. When those guys start talking, it's just too fast for me."

"No. I can manage."

Zoey visibly relaxed. "Well, you do speak it like a native."

"I've no doubt she does, but she'll want moral support," Eleanor said.

"Please no," Isobella looked up, for the first time making eye contact. "I can manage and I don't want to spoil your evening."

"Our evening is of no matter," Eleanor assured her.

"I think I will keep my cool if I go alone," Isobella started weakly. "You girls will bring out the emotions in me. I need to keep a level head, so I might help the police as much as I can. For Alberto."

"Did you want a glass of water?" Rosemary appeared in the doorway with a tumbler of ice and water.

Eleanor gave her a taught smile. "Thank you." She put the glass on Isobella's night stand. "Honey, if you're sure you're ok going on your own."

"I am."

"What's going on?" Rosemary looked bewildered.

"Please, go on to the jazz cafe. I'll join you as soon as I can."

"All right. But we won't take offence if you don't turn up. You might not feel like it after you've been to the police."

Eleanor took Rosemary by the elbow to her own room to quietly explain what had happened. Zoey, feeling awkward, went down to her own flat to wait for the girls. Isobella tied her hair back in a functional fashion and took off her earrings. She put a few things in her handbag.

108

The four girls left the apartment block together and separated at the end of the lane, Zoey, Eleanor and Rosemary to the club, Isobella in the direction of the police station, a folded newspaper in her hand. With a few drinks and the company of handsome men, the girls relaxed and enjoyed the conversation and music. They didn't see Isobella, and got home late, going straight to bed. It was Saturday the next day and Isobella wasn't up. They guessed it had been a long night for her too, and she would be tired and grieving. In the early afternoon Eleanor went in with a cup of coffee to see how she was, perhaps offer a sympathetic ear. It didn't work out like that.

Rosemary approached her sister, confused by the way she just stood in the open doorway. "What's going on?"

She looked into the room. It was tidy. The bed made and unslept in. The dressing table and nightstand had been cleared, and the books that used to rest on the windowsill tided away. When they dared to go in and start opening cupboards and drawers, they realised that all personal items had been removed. Isobella had gone.

By the time the young American women had explained their story succinctly to the Italian police; Isobella had crossed the border into Switzerland. And when the police contacted Interpol, embarrassed about the details they were communicating, she was in Austria. Although by that point she had crossed the border as Isobella Omnes, thanks to a high quality counterfeit British passport purchased in Switzerland.

It was difficult for the Italian inspector to make any real progress on the case, and eventually the murder of Alberto Montebruno, surgical extraordinaire never to be, was filed away in the depths of the Genoa police archives. Some facts were clear. He had died on a Saturday from a single, confident slice across the neck. A few hours prior to death he had been at a nearby *ristorante* with a pretty, dark haired woman. The couple had driven off on his Vespa, which was found abandoned by the side of the road in the hills. No one ever saw Alberto again. Alive at least. At the very minimum the woman knew who had killed him, but the inspector suspected she was involved. There were similarities in the single slash of death, as well as the hidden away nature of the place where the body was found, the state of undress as though the passions of love had been completed. And of course the highly implicating fact that this woman had disappeared the very day she learned the body had been discovered.

The American girl had recognised Alberto, and she claimed he was the boyfriend of the woman who lived in the apartment upstairs. She had even seen the two of them riding off from the seafront on Alberto's Vespa that fateful Saturday at noon.

It was at this point that the case became laughable. Take the description, for instance. The *ristorante* owner, the Americans, the colleagues at the office; they all agreed. A beautiful young woman with long dark hair. Highly desirable. What a wonderful description. It would evoke a different image in every man's mind, and quite frankly described a large proportion of the Mediterranean female population. There were no photos of the woman in anyone's possession, not even the young lover's student room. That very fact was at first surprising, but if this woman was an experienced killer, she would have known to cover her tracks.

Even worse was her name. Isobella Donagh. To his ears it sounded as Isobella Donna. He had stared at the American girl. Really? Yes, but a lot of people called her Bella. He was expected to put out a trace on a mysteriously beautiful woman called Bella Donna? Keep your eyes open, men, she could be anywhere. In truth she was everywhere. She spoke excellent Italian but was actually French, according to the American.

That was all he had. The Americans would be able to identify her if the police ever picked her up. But it would never happen. There was no French citizen called Bella Donna. They never did get the spelling of her name correct on the forms, actually Isobella Donagh. And by the time she entered Austria, she was Isobella Omnes of Great Britain. Taking her mother's maiden name was a half truth, but it was enough for her to completely disappear without a trace.

The episode had woken Isobella up to the fact of what a dangerous game she had been playing. She had been toying with her liberty, taking such risks with the laws of the land. Prison and captivity was something she would not survive. On the train into Austria, she had gazed out of the window and gone into a cold sweat at the thought of being forever separated from her tincture. Never again to walk barefoot in the forest. It was strange, considering the death that had almost tripped her up had been the only one committed whilst utterly sober. Usually she was high on her drug.

As frightening as it all was, and as confused Alberto's words had left her, it was not the end. Isobella still took trips with her tincture and she still took men's lives. She could not even explain it to herself anymore. Some seemed apathetic to death, others terrified. Some deserved it; others had things left to do. It didn't matter. There was no logic. Only the beat of the tincture and the earthly feeling that this was her purpose.

So she drifted. Sometimes she only stayed for a few days, other times for months on end. She criss crossed her way through Austria, learning the language of German, fitting in with that corner of the world. From the Alps she travelled up through West Germany, skirting across into both Belgium and Holland as she went, before going up through Denmark and over the short crossing by boat into Southern Sweden. It was in Sweden that an opportunity arose to take her aimless travelling to the next level.

She was living in Stockholm at this time and had been taken up by a rather intense young man. He was serious, suited and very involved in a blossoming career in government, but when he had set eyes on Isobella Omnes, something had flicked on in his brain and he could not let her alone. He was a man obsessed.

They didn't live together, although he would often visit her and spend the night. She had taken drops an hour or so ago when he turned up at her flat late one evening. Her eyes were still dilated and she was getting too much light from the moon. All the lights in the flat were off. He had entered a rather ethereal atmosphere. Almost like secondary smoking, he had somehow imbibed of her hallucinogenics as they both seemed to float away. He was absorbed by her. Isobella had decided to end it in her permanent way of things, when he had brought up his suggestion. Her fingers had relaxed around the knife handle, before slipping the weapon back underneath the book as she listened to the details.

Sören worked in the diplomatic core, and he was being posted abroad. His managers were so happy with his work that he was going to a much envied posting, the United States of America. He was going to work in the Swedish embassy in Washington D.C. He was intensely excited about the opportunity, but there was one lock on his enthusiasm which meant he wasn't sure if he would be able to go. One thing that was holding him back in Sweden. He wanted her to go with him.

Legs akimbo across him, Isobella sat back on her haunches, putting pressure on his pelvis as he made the suggestion. Move to America with him. Move to America. She'd read so much about the place, seen so much on the television. Heard the music, seen the films. And of course met the Americans themselves who flooded Europe. Yet the idea of travelling anywhere that was so far away, so distantly unconnected by land mass to where she had been before, had simply never occurred to her. Isobella had no plans, but there was still a lot of Europe she hadn't wandered through in search of belonging.

America was the new land. People from all countries went there to start new lives. Perhaps that was the place for her.

From her hunched position on the windowsill Isobella caught sight of herself in the mirror on the wall. It was the only item actually hanging in the room. The other decoration consisted of a painting straight on to the plaster, screaming about free love and drugs in rainbow colours. According to local lore, a girl had painted it a couple of years ago before disappearing off to the west coast. Isobella had been living in this room for four months. She was starting to get that itchy feet feeling. She certainly didn't belong here, and perhaps it was time to try somewhere new.

It had been three years since she had first come to the United States of America. She'd only stayed with her Swedish diplomat a couple of months, before packing her sparse belongings one evening whilst he was out at a formal dinner. She had gone when he returned in the small hours of the morning, no forwarding address left.

She'd moved around a lot, and in truth this was the country where such a rootless existence felt most natural. She had bought a cheap car and travelled around the northern states, focusing in particular on Michigan, Minnesota and Wisconsin. She'd worked in little offices and diners, and spent a lot of time in the forests and by the great lakes. Such intense volumes of water, but not a crystal of salt. It was like being at the ocean, and yet she knew across the far side there was Canada. This was wilderness on a scale she had not seen before. She would go out for days, sometimes weeks at a time, to live in the forests, to take her tincture and to travel to a higher level of consciousness. She'd see other hikers and campers occasionally, either letting them pass or picking them off on something of a whim. It was on one particular attempt that she was surprised when she discovered what she had thought was a solitary man by the fire was actually part of a group, his comrades splashed out on the ground like stranded starfish. They were all high on LSD and tripping through their own individual nightmares and paradises. Only the man sat on the log had any awareness left, choosing instead to sit and smoke pot. Perhaps he was the designated responsible one. In such company, a girl with highly dilated eyes and a spaced out demeanour was hardly out of place and no one even realised she may have taken something.

Isobella had never killed a woman before – there were two in the party – and she'd certainly never taken on a group. Although her experiences in Europe hadn't stopped the apathetic lust for blood, it had made her cautious. Witnesses were not an option, so she had carefully slipped the knife back into her bag. Even high on tincture she knew when she was outnumbered. She had sat down on the log by the man and listened to him talk. They were on holiday to commune with nature before heading back to the village, and hey, she looked like a cool kind of chick, she should go with them.

So she was now here in the village, a tongue in cheek name perhaps for a great sprawling suburban section of the massive concrete jungle that was New York. Despite the metropolis there was a village feel, for in this tumble of artists, musicians and drug-addled hippies, there was a sense of community and a comfort that everyone knew everyone else. Isobella was the bewildered explorer who had somehow fallen into this society. She'd taken a small room in a shared flat where they didn't pay rent because the girl with the best room paid the landlord in sexual favours. And she liked having her roommates, hey, she needed the company.

To some extent Isobella had changed, thoughtlessly merging to match her cohorts. She had a thick fringe in her hair, wore a red neckerchief that an intense communist had given her a couple of parties ago. He was still trying to get into her bed, and he would eventually succeed only to have his body discovered in a dumpster the next day – case never solved.

There was music playing in the room next door, or rather music was being played. It was a thoughtful thrumming through the guitar strings. She stood up and wandered through to the neighbouring room where a dark-haired, dark-eyed boy from New Jersey was sitting on the floor singing to himself. He'd arrived a month ago to bring his art to the masses, and was currently working through a song. Notes and sheets littered the floor in front of him. To the side there was a full ashtray with a smoking splif balanced on the rim. He looked up as Isobella entered the room, and hummed as he ran through a number of chords. He took up the splif and sucked on the hazy mist before offering it to Isobella.

She shook her head as she sat down on the floor before him.

"You don't do drugs really," he commented, setting the homemade cigarette back in the ashtray. "I've noticed. And yet you do get high. You're on something but you don't share." His fingers flicked back across the neck of the guitar as he sang the final comment: "What is it you do Bella Bella?"

It wasn't something she talked about with people. She shrugged. "No name. My own brew. Everyone has their own poison."

He nodded. He was only in his early twenties and yet he felt as though he was weighted down with the wisdom of the world. "Will you listen to this song?" he asked. "I've been finishing it today. I'm working on a collection. I'm going to record an album. I think this would be a good opener."

"Sure." Isobella lay back, pulling across a floor cushion to rest her head on. She closed her eyes as she listened to him play, gentle vocals murmuring along to the melody. When he was finished, she said nothing, and looked to all appearances as though she was in a deep sleep.

He put the guitar to one side. "Hey, I think I want to get high with you."

She opened her eyes a crack. "You can get high, but I'm not taking anything."

"I mean the stuff you use."

"I don't think you'd cope with it."

"I would. Just give me a chance."

He looked earnestly at her, and for a change Isobella thought why not? It was impulsive, perhaps foolish, but she would not be here that much longer. She sat up. "All right. Tip your head back."

"Tip my head back?" He watched as she pulled out the necklace that hung under her top. There was a vial as a pendant.

"You take it through the eyes."

"The eyes," he whispered. "The windows on the soul."

He wasn't quite so poetic when the single drops met with the surface of the eye and forced his pupils to rapidly dilate. For a first timer it could be painful, followed by a second hit through light sensitivity. He gasped and dry-wretched, rolling on to his side.

Isobella moved across to him, manoeuvring him to the mattress on the floor before taking a dose herself and emptying the vial.

"I think it's something of an acquired taste."

"I don't even know what I'm seeing. I feel my heart is sprinting." He felt her move across him more than he saw, and rather boldly put his hands up her top. They didn't exchange any more words, but simply coupled on the dirty mattress on the floor. Isobella had already decided she wouldn't take his life. She felt there was a lot of goodness to come out of this one, and she liked his music. It would be a shame to finish it before he'd even recorded his first album.

The following day he skulked behind sunglasses, fuzzy headed. He was still not quite sure what had happened yesterday. Isobella gave no clue of anything out of the ordinary.

"Hey, Bella," The girl with the best room caught her in the kitchen. "I need to ask a favour. My cousin is flying back today and I promised to pick him up from Idlewild."

"Idlewild?"

She rolled her eyes. "Man, I keep forgetting and it's not like it happened yesterday. JFK Airport, of course. You know what I'm talking about. I've got to fetch him but my ride fell through. Would you drive me out there? Bring us back?"

Isobella shrugged. "Sure."

The girl chattered incessantly during the drive out to JFK airport. She'd heard that Isobella had gotten high with her neighbour yesterday, and they'd taken something heavy. Far Out. He still looked frazzled. His eyes could barely cope with looking at reality again. The light. The light. When they arrived and parked up Isobella couldn't remember much of what had been said, other than that this nameless cousin was coming back from England. 'My cousin' she said, as if this man were property, or that the possession might transfer the glory of success to herself. Another singer songwriter, for the new folk scene was booming. He'd been touring and experiencing another country, but had decided the time was ripe to come back home and start hitting the big time.

The girls entered the arrivals hall. It was an international burble of people, echoing back up in the dizzy heights of the open roof plan. Helvetica signs to direct people onwards to their destinations. Families and friends reuniting. Tired and weary travellers setting foot on American soil and just wanting to sleep. The girl spun around, her open sheepskin coat spreading out like the wings of a bird. Her feathered hair floated around her face and she grinned at Isobella. "I have no idea where he might be. You wait here. I'm going to take a look."

Isobella shrugged, disinterested, and was abandoned in the multitude of strangers. Languages, some familiar, some not, washed over her. She stared at nothing, her hands nonchalantly in her trouser pockets.

"*Mama mia!*" A woman shouted in the crowds of arriving people, a greeting much louder than the majority. A few groups of people stopped talking and looked across at her.

"I don't believe it," she continued, leaving her travelling companions and elbowing her way through the crowds. Isobella glanced over as she realised the woman was heading in her direction.

"Isobella? Isobella Donagh? It's been a long time."

She looked blankly at the woman in front of her, her brain making no sense of what she saw. A woman in her fifties with thickly curled and styled hair that came down just shy of her shoulders. There were many clumps of grey twisted through what was once the darkest of brown hair. She a rounded woman, her waist merged into her hips and chest. She wore a deep mauve dress and jacket, with a thick and fluffy fur wrap that beefed up around her shoulders. She reached out with a hand adorned with bright diamond rings and touched Isobella's forearm. Her eyes narrowed slightly to take a better look, the laughter lines deepening.

"It's Rosa. You remember me?"

Isobella looked perplexed.

"We worked as translators together in Britain, during the war. You disappeared into Wales..." Her story drifted off as she got her glasses out of her handbag and put them on. Now that she took a detailed look at the woman she was beginning to realise she must have made a mistake, and yet it was as though they were back in London. Sharing a room when Isobella's own lodgings had been destroyed in a bombing raid. But it couldn't be Isobella Donagh. Not unless Isobella had stepped through a time warp direct from the Blitz to this very day, getting a contemporary fringe cut on the way.

"Honey, what's your mother called?"

"Ahes."

Rosa's hopeful smile started to fade. "Your family name?"

"Omnes."

"Oh, I am sorry. You just looked the spit of a girl I used to know, I almost fell over."

Isobella stared at her, knocking the extra weight and the years off, smoothing out the skin and darkening the hair. Throwing that ugly fur across the room. Filtering through the names and faces she had known, making her journey back through Europe till she returned to London.

"Of course, you couldn't be her," Rosa continued, warmly. "It's been over twenty years since I last saw Isobella, and honey, she was a looker but nobody ages that well. I wondered if you might be her daughter, but that would have been too much of a coincidence."

A well dressed gent in his fifties appeared beside Rosa. They both looked like middle aged money, comfortable from a successful business and life. "Honey, the car's waiting," he said, taking Rosa's forearm in that familiar manner. "Is this a friend of yours?"

"No," Rosa smiled sadly. "Just a doppelganger. We've never met before. I'm sorry I bothered you. Have a nice day." She walked away with her husband, shaking her head to herself. "It's just uncanny," she told him. "Like seeing a ghost from my past."

They had both just seen ghosts. Rosa followed a cynics' path and disproved the experience to herself. Isobella was reeling from what she had just seen. It was ridiculous, but when she left a place she forgot about the people she had known, consigning them to another chapter of her life, and just assuming on some level that they ceased to exist. Frozen memories and nothing more.

"Bella, bella, there you are!" The girl scampered back to her flatmate. "You've got to meet my cousin," she added, gleefully grabbing his arm and pushing him forward. "Fresh from Great Britain."

"Hey there, Bella," the dark haired cousin greeted her. "I'm Anthony."

"Your name isn't Anthony!" the girl shrieked in amusement.

"Today it is. I'm jetlagged. I'm told you've got us a ride into town?"

Isobella nodded. "Sure. Let's go."

Isobella moved through a dream for the next few weeks. Rosa. Britain. Her past. She was so focused on finding somewhere she belonged, she'd forgotten about all that went before. Lost in her memories, she barely noticed the present. When she took the communist's life, she was hardly aware of what she was doing, thoughtlessly dragging his discarded body to the dumpster. It was pure good fortune that no one saw her.

Standing in her room, feeling the first effects of the tincture, she gazed at herself in the mirror. Her reflection was swallowed up by the deep expanse of her dilated eyes. Who am I? I am myself. Or am I my own daughter? Time had passed, not just days and weeks, but years and decades. Who am I? Where do I belong?

The radio was on playing a song about wearing flowers in your hair. It had come out a year or two ago, but the broadcasting stations still couldn't get enough. Isobella pressed her forehead to the cool glass of the mirror. "San Francisco," she whispered to herself. She was going to San Francisco.

Isobella got to San Francisco although it took her a couple of years to arrive. Driving east to west in America was no small undertaking. Coupled to this was the fact that she did not take a straight line. She ambled through the states, stopping off now and then. Sometimes she'd stay somewhere a day or two, sometimes a month. Seasons passed by. Isobella lost track of time. New York City was back there in another closed chapter, and there was no deadline on opening up the section marked San Francisco. There was no rush at all.

She arrived with the May riots as people protested against the government's seeming extension of an unpopular war out in Asia. Countries and cultures she'd never seen and could barely imagine: Vietnam, Laos, Cambodia. Disconnected as she was, Isobella did not worry about these international events. She listened to people discuss wars and politics, human rights and free love with only half an ear. She travelled up and down the hills of the city, riding the city trams, oblivious to the eyes that stared at her.

The red neckerchief had been lost somewhere in Nebraska. She'd stopped cutting her fringe, and now had two bangs framing her face down to her jaw line. She wore long, full length cotton dresses of intense colours, adorned with strings of cheap beads. She moved into a flat with three long haired men, who were all keen to add a woman to their community for different reasons. Two of the men were lovers, although it was still five years shy of such love being legalised in California. A woman gave a heterosexual validation to the group even though she was never more than a platonic addition. The third man was a mystery, deep inside he hid the heart of a misogynist. Why he had been living with the couple, or why he so eagerly agreed to Isobella moving in, would never be clear. He sat and made plans that never really came to fruition. Perhaps he would have succeeded, only that a few months into the new living arrangements, it was suggested they go on a road trip. Nothing was the same afterwards.

David, making up one half of a couple with Leonard, was a great pot head. He was convinced there was a better brand to be purchased in Mexico, and over the course of a few weeks persuaded the singles; Mac and Isobella, that all four of them ought to take a late summer holiday. They could drive down to Mexico, get over the border, and get really high. Leonard had heard about peyote, some Latin American cactus that the shamans used to use, and was keen to go try it in the 'homeland' as he called it, despite the fact that none of them had any connection to Mexico. Isobella's car, with a clock of hundreds of thousands of miles, had given up and she had sold it to a mechanic for spare parts. Who knew what he would make of the worn out heap, but he hadn't been able to turn away that face without making an offer.

With money in her pocket and all her possessions she intended to keep bagged up, Isobella joined the three men in the VW campervan. They were planning on coming back, little did they know that Isobella, last to leave the flat, had cleared out her presence and had no intention of returning. Latin America was calling.

They drove in state, across the continent, to make a 'real journey' of it, before crossing the border down at El Paso and into the Mexican countryside. Isobella was in the campervan, feet propped up on a spare seat, reading a dog-eared copy of 'Teach Yourself Spanish'. Mac sweated in a corner and fanaticised about what he was going to do to here when he got the chance. Up front David and Leonard bickered. Leonard was convinced they were in the right part of the country. They were going to be shamans. It was all going to be good.

They drove through a flat, dry arid landscape. Blue skies, hints of hills in the distance. Scrubby dry bushes covered the earth in patches. They were driving Route 45 for what felt like hours without seeing a damned town. The sun beat down on the metal van. Sweat beaded on foreheads. Tempers frayed.

As dusk fell they drove into a low lying little town, Villa Ahumada. Plastered one storey buildings, empty plots. Locals roaming the streets. They got lost, turning off from the main roads and the line of the railway, instead ending up on some dark little backstreet. As the engine was turned off the sound was replaced with the hopeless barking of dogs somewhere in the slumbering sprawl of desert habitation.

"Man, look, there's a bar over there," David, ever the optimist, pointed. "A bit of real local culture. None of that tourist crap."

"Maybe they'll know about the shamans."

"Let's get ourselves a couple of *cervezas* and then figure out where the hell we are."

They got out of the van. A couple of children who had been out on the street ran into a nearby building. After a moment or two bright eyes dared to stare out again at the strange motor vehicle that had arrived. Americans. They didn't usually come to this part of town.

Isobella followed the men towards the bar, lifting her eyes to gaze up at the sky. It felt old here, intensely dark beyond the badly wired electric lights. Spanish was spoken. Nasal American English had no home. The men ahead sounded and looked very out of place.

"You've been reading that book all day," David called back to her. "Maybe you can ask for directions."

Inside the bar groups of men sat around small tables, or lounged against the walls drinking beer. A ceiling fan fought in vain against the heat. Electric lights hummed and flickered. There was a bottled intensity of sweat and alcohol. A pretty girl in a white blouse and heavy skirts was collecting empty bottles. The bar man, a swarthy dark man with a sun-creased face and deep moustache, paused in wiping down glasses as the strangers entered. It was a clichéd moment; talk of the day ceased as something a little out of the ordinary strolled into the bar.

David and Leonard, innocents of the world, strolled up with silly smiles on their faces. "*Hombre*," they greeted the man. "*Dos cervezas.*"

"There's four of us here," Mac growled.

David looked sheepish. "I only count to three." He looked back at the bar man who had still yet to move a move or say anything. "*Dos y dos.*"

The barkeeper set a tequila glass upside down on the bar and regarded the three males. He barked out a few lines that had a couple of the regulars sniggering. It was a guttural, fast Spanish that the Americans didn't understand. Isobella listened to the voices around her. Spanish was close enough to her French and Italian for her to understand, although it would take her a little while to pick up the colloquialisms of Mexico.

No alcohol was forthcoming. David and Leonard looked uncertainly at one another.

"They're just dumb tourists." Isobella stepped up behind the men, speaking in fast Spanish. She had a slight French lilt that the locals took for her being from Europe, but aside from that, they understood one another. "They just want to drink some beer and spend their American dollars with you. They're really not worth getting angry about."

The barman abruptly broke out into an alarming grin that was probably meant to be reassuring, but had a slightly devilish look about it. He pointed at Isobella. "*Chica.*" The atmosphere relaxed, the tension that had been pulling taught between the walls as if to crush them all, suddenly going slack. The barman looked to the three Americans. "You pay dollars."

The international language of money. And with a couple of drinks everyone was friends. David and Leonard grinned. "Sure man. Now let's have some drinks."

Grinning and laughter went a long way, even when there was virtually no shared language. Each nationality had a few words of one another's mother tongue, but certainly not enough to string a conversation together. But as the evening drew on the tourists melted into the local clientele, and there was much laughter as the locals and the strangers talked at each other, for the most part having no real idea what was being said. Isobella remained as an observer, understanding both sides but having no real inclination to join in. David and Leonard were having a great time making new friends. Mac didn't join in so much, occasionally leaning in for a comment or two, but for the most part he had his eyes on the barmaid. He tried to catch her eye and talk to her whenever she was passing, but she appeared to have even less English than the barman, and didn't dare look him in the eye. As the drinks went down his throat Mac looked like he felt he had more to prove.

It was nearing midnight when Isobella noted the barmaid slipping out of the front entrance, although whether to take a break or head home she couldn't say. It seemed strange that such a sweet looking girl would be working somewhere like this. And yet none of the regulars caused her any trouble. She gazed through the smoky fug, guessing that a brother or two were in here, and everyone else knew it.

The glasses on her little table wobbled as Mac stretched out his legs, carelessly knocking at the table. Bottles and glasses, short and tall, clinked against one another. "Watch it, man," Leonard drawled, a cigarette dangling from the corner of his mouth as he caught a couple of glasses from tumbling off the edge of the table.

"I need some air," Mac muttered as he stood up. "Just stepping out."

Isobella lowered her head and ran her hands down the sides of her thighs to check the contents of her pockets through the dress fabric. She had an uneasy feeling. She knew what Mac was going out for, and she didn't think that girl would be able to defend herself. On the other hand this sort of thing happened all the time across the world, and who was she to play God and say what was right. She remembered being back in Italy, in Genoa in the flat that final night. Looking out of the window at the family across the way, the husband regularly beating his wife. The kind of man whom she supposed deserved to die, rather than that beautiful trainee doctor she had taken on a whim. Isobella's moral

126

compass was skewed and rarely functioning, but today it was juddering.

She stood up.

Beyond the halos thrown out from the lamps it was black as if nothing else existed outside. The air was at a comfortable temperature. Isobella stood on the dusty road by the bar. A dog howled somewhere in the night. Disembodied. Something whimpered. A glass broke.

Her footsteps gently crunched as she paced along the front of the Mexican bar to the side alley that ran down between it and the next building. She stood, emotionless, and watched. A slight breeze rippled through her long dress and her waist-length black hair. The little barmaid's face was now streaked with tears, a grimace to her expression. She was pushed up against the wall, bloodied fingers scrabbling uselessly against the plasterwork. Her skirts were hauled up to her waist. Mac was behind her, gripping onto her hair with one hand as if he would otherwise blow away with the wind. With the other he was trying to get his belt unbuckled.

Isobella coughed and started to walk up to them. Mac looked up at the distraction. The barmaid felt the lapse in concentration and made a bolt to get away. She wasn't quick enough, or perhaps she would never have managed, for his fingers were like a vice through her hair. Mac grinned, assuming this was a kind of warped jealously and he'd finally gotten a reaction out of Isobella. "You want to watch, sweetheart?"

The barmaid opened her mouth to plead in Spanish with Isobella. Mac went to grab at her as if he would be able to control two women at once, bend them both over for his amusement. Isobella moved so quickly it would have been easy to convince oneself that she had never actually made a move. Certainly never attacked. That knife had stayed in her pocket. It had not fallen into the comfortable hold in her hand, the blade flicked out. It was a slash through the air, the well sharpened blade whipping through skin and flesh. Her hand was at her side again. A line welled up across Mac's throat, and for a moment it looked as though nothing more would happen. Then the blood started to pour. Thick heavy pulsations pushed through the gap to gush down his chest.

The barmaid gasped and whimpered, staggering away as his iron hold faltered. She ran, sobbing, and got out into the middle of the road. "*Senorita*," she said, as if worried for Isobella's safety.

Mac staggered towards her, opening his mouth to curse her, but the air gargled in his own blood. He roughly stepped up, colliding with her. Wet warm blood slapped up against her, drenching the front of her dress and making the fabric stick to her skin. Isobella put a finger to his chest and gently pushed. He fell back into the dirt.

Isobella turned around and stepped back into the half light of the road. She felt the wind sweep up around her ankles. She stood numb and emotionless. She wasn't quite sure what to do now. She never had killed without consummation before. Completely sober and no coming. This was a very unsettling experience.

"Hey, Isobella, where'd you get to?" Leonard wandered out of the bar as if in a daze. He stopped when he saw the crying Mexican barmaid, his eyes drifting across to his flatmate. A thick splash of blood down her front. She looked as though she had been attacked. "What happened, are you all right?" He moved forward a few steps before faltering. He couldn't say if it was the expression on her face or the fact that Mac's body lay inert behind her with a growing dark pool in the dirt, that assured him she was not wounded.

"Oh man," Leonard groaned. "What did you do?"

The barmaid started babbling, but Leonard couldn't understand her. The noise brought a few of the locals out of the bar. The girl ran to the barman as he appeared, eyes flickering from figure to figure as he listened to her account, coolly understanding what had happened.

"Isobella, what have you done?" Leonard shouted. "We came here to get high. Not to kill Mac."

She widened her eyes. "Go."

"You can't..." Leonard's words were stopped by a heavy hand on his shoulder. He looked up at the barman.

"You and he go," he said. "Now."

David was in the crowd spilling from the bar. "What's happening? Leonard? Oh shit..." he saw Isobella.

Leonard grabbed his arm. "We have to get out of here." He pushed David towards the camper van.

"What about Isobella? Where's Mac? She's been attacked."

"David, just get in the fucking van," Leonard hissed. His hands were shaking violently. "We have to go right now."

The barman, clearly the authority figure of this street, walked up to Isobella. The barmaid was clinging onto his arm. "*Chica*," he said. Isobella was staring straight through him. Was this shock from what she had just done? He wasn't particularly bothered about the dead man, from what he'd heard, he deserved it. He clicked his fingers in front of the woman's eyes. Her pupils flickered and she focused on his face, registering what he was saying.

"We don't know what was between you and that fucker," he spoke to her in Spanish. "And we don't care. You did my sister a big favour. But you've got to get out of here. You're in trouble now, you understand. This isn't some dead Mexican after some bar fight. This is an American you killed, you understand? The cops here are going to care. And when his momma and papa back home find out, the American cops are going to care. You've got to put some distance between you and that dead motherfucker." He glanced down at her body. "And you've got to burn that dress."

Leonard had taken Isobella's carpet bag and handbag out of the van and set them down on the road. He scrambled back into the driver's seat and the vehicle raced down the street.

Her mind was starting to catch up with the situation. She couldn't go back to the States. She had to move, she had to go deeper into Mexico. She had to disappear. She started to walk, heading for her belongings. The other men from the bar parted willingly for her. No one wanted to get to close to the crazy woman. She picked up her bags.

"I have no wheels."

As she turned back, the barman took a set of keys out of his pocket and threw them to her. "I owe you this, and that is all." He pointed down the street at a car. "It's a piece of shit, but it'll get you out of here."

"What will you do?" Her eyes flickered to Mac's body.

"We'll deal with it," he said grimly. "And you were never here."

And so Isobella Donagh, known as Isobella Omnes, disappeared into Latin America. She dumped the barman's car as soon as it ran out of fuel and wandered out into the wilderness. She burned all of her clothes from the night of the murder when it got dark, took her tincture and leapt around in the desert, gasping and drowning in amazement under the endless spread of stars.

The next morning she'd dressed with fresh clothes out of her bag, then started walking. She hitched a lift when she next reached a road and travelled into the heart of Mexico, imitating the dialect from the talkative drivers who gave her lifts and the locals she listened to when she stopped in towns and villages. The heat and the sun tanned her skin, the temperature embodying her with a permanent shining sweat. Her hair thickened and coiled like a long black snake down her back.

She achieved David's ambition on his behalf when she met three old sisters. They lived on the edge of an isolated village and had a reputation for second sight. It turned out they had quite a little rock garden of peyote and were well aware of the cactus' hallucinogenic properties. She spent a couple of months with the women, becoming part of the sibling community, learning their ways and learning their lore. The sisters, who had never been more than fifty miles from this family stone cottage, were fascinated to hear of Europe, of the green forests, the constant rain, and of the Breton culture and those secrets Ahes had taught her.

For a long time Isobella did not take a life. She wondered if she had broken a pattern of behaviour, or a force of habit that she had lived with for as long as she could remember. But she had not chosen a good time to enter Central America. These were the violent times of guerrillas and socialist rebels, dictatorships and unforgiving regimes, people who were kidnapped and tortured or simply disappeared in the night and were never heard of again. They were unstable times and hardly the safest for a single woman to travel aimlessly, even if she could quickly pick up the local dialects and convince people of her native status. She saw poverty and wide eyed starving children. Frightened women. Emboldened young men holding rifles whilst posing at the side of the homestead. They were fighting for the people. She wondered about that communist back in New York, and how he would have coped in this reality, where there was real fighting, death and injury and not enough to eat. She saw terrible injuries come back from the jungles, gun shots and machete hacks, infections and oozing wounds that would not heal in the tropical humid temperature. She dodged bullets, and learned to hide from the authorities. She listened to the jungle, and learned the signs of nature from the environment, where to find food and water, when to know that trouble was approaching. She let roaming hands come upon her and listened patiently to the passionate speeches of the rebels and the idealists. When she was caught out or in a position of non consent, she would whip out the knife and quickly clear herself of the problem. Being a lone female frequently worked in her favour, for so many men never thought that she could ever be a danger to them in any respect.

She made it through the arm of Central America and into the north of South America, staying at villages and towns, seeing the drug cartels destroy the lives of the communities. None of it seemed to be about the higher experience and mind expansion, rather just guns and profits. She entered Brazil at a watershed when the military rule ended and civilian government took control. There were new experiences for all, and after many years of Spanish she had a new language to learn. She stayed in Manaus on the banks of the Rio Negro for almost a year. It was a flat lying city of paint-peeling shanty towns, water and boats and the ever growing vegetation.

She roamed the continent without awareness of direction or time. Had she a GPS locator, it would have tracked a confused rambling path over South America, routes curling and crossing back over themselves. She made her way through the mighty Brazil, dropping through Paraguay and into Argentina. She was swept up with the dances and the music, travelling through the country to the city of Buenos Aires, then gradually back out into the countryside, sometimes on foot, sometimes hitching rides, or by horseback. Ever roaming without aim or hope, thinking there was nothing to be found that would snap her out of this endless daze.

This came to a surprising halt near to the coast in a town called Gaiman. This was where she entered the Y Wladfa, and suddenly, inexplicably she was back home. The familiarity was like an electric shock, so sudden and unexpected. Yet there it was. In the medley of heat, great plains, Spanish and the tango, there was Cymraeg. There was Welsh.

Her brain short circuited when she heard Welsh being spoken, fluent and comfortable, but with its own local twist, because this was now a homebrew of a very different environment to the little country far away over the Atlantic. Isobella passed out cold in the middle of the street.

She woke up to the light breeze of the Rio Chubut and the sound of the wind rustling through the tree lined roads of Gaiman. Her head felt like lead, as if she was coming out of the heavy fog of tincture. She squinted into the room, recognising nothing. She lay on a big double bed, floor length white curtains gently billowing at the window. The room was sparsely decorated. There were no features to offer a clue as to who lived there, but it was clean and tidy. Isobella sat up and coughed. She felt as though she was suffering from amnesia.

"You are well?" a female voice asked in uncomfortable Welsh.

She stiffened, surprised that there was another in the room.

"I wonder, I sorry..." the Welsh faltered as a young woman stepped forward from the side of the room. She wore a neat dress of pale blue with an embroidered pattern around the hemline. Her hair was tied up in a bun. Blonde hair, but olive Hispanic skin and green eyes. She shook her head as if to say it was no good. "¿Hablas español?" she queried, admitting defeat and returning to what was comfortable.

Isobella put her hand to her forehead. "Yes," she replied in Spanish. "Of course I speak Spanish. How can I be here and not speak it?"

The stranger seemed to relax. She nodded. "You're Argentinean? You sound it. But you were..."

"I was?"

She fiddled with her fingers. "I should explain. You had passed out on the street. Maybe it was the heat. We brought you in here to rest. It's a guesthouse, my family's business."

That would explain the room and the lack of personal decoration. There was probably a line of similar rooms surrounding this cell.

Isobella swung her legs over the side of the bed. "I must thank you for your kindness, Miss, er..."

"My name is Lopez, Juanita Lopez."

"Nice to meet you. Isobella."

"Ah, Isobella."

"I should not trespass on your hospitality any longer."

"It has been a great curiosity for us since you came here," Juanita burst out as Isobella moved as if to dash up from the bed. "You sounded delirious. You've been sleeping and talking whilst you were unconscious. You spoke Welsh."

"Yes, of course," Isobella breathed, starting to remember. She looked back sharply at the girl. "I heard Welsh spoken, in the town."

She smiled simply. "We speak it here. Well, some do. I don't speak it so well. My mother was not so diligent in my lessons when I was a child, and of course Papa only speaks Spanish, so..." she shrugged as if that explained her own history enough. "You're not from this region, eh? You didn't know about the Welsh communities? They came here in the 1800s."

"I didn't know."

"But you were speaking Welsh. I mean, fluently. Better than I can. But you don't come from here. I don't understand."

"I come from Wales." The statement was out of her mouth before she had chance to consider it. Although she had grown up in the land of dragons, she had always considered herself Breton. It had been decades since she'd last seen Wales. Yet now that the words were out, it felt right.

"You talk Spanish like a local, if you don't mind me saying."

"I have an affinity for languages."

"Yes, there was something else you were speaking. Something strange. I don't know what it was, but my grandfather said he knows."

"Your grandfather?"

"Yes, he knew what you were speaking. He said to come and see him when you're better."

"Oh." Isobella looked around the room, worrying what she might have been saying in her sleep.

"He's just downstairs."

She considered fleeing, for there was always a risk she'd made some terrible confession that she did not want to have to explain. Isobella had a great many secrets she needed to keep. Juanita looked very keen for her to go downstairs, and she supposed they had done her a good turn by taking her in off the streets. "I'm well," she said, standing up from the bed. "Let's go meet your grandfather."

Through to the private apartments of the building, there was a high ceiling living room with large doors and windows looking out onto a veranda and beyond to a garden. At the far end, set by the open French windows was a winged armchair with an old man. He had a woven blanket spread out across his legs. Even in this warmth he felt a chill. He put down his book down as the two women entered the room.

"Grandfather," Juanita approached. "Our guest is awake now. Isobella," she looked back over her shoulder. "This is my grandfather."

"Ah, Isobella," the old man nodded, now able to put a name to the face. "Welcome to our humble home. It's a guesthouse and today you are our guest. I think Juanita will have told you that you fainted outside? We were happy to help you in this crisis." He spoke fluent Spanish, but there was a definite accent she couldn't place.

He regarded her for a moment. "Or would you prefer if we spoke in Welsh?" he asked, this time picking up the old Celtic tongue.

Isobella was still disorientated. Even with his Welsh there was an accent.

"Isobella speaks beautiful Spanish," Juanita said. "I thought she was Argentinean."

"And she speaks Welsh, for we heard it," he told his granddaughter. "Will you fetch us something to drink? I want to talk to this woman." He gestured to a seat beside him as Juanita left the room.

Isobella sat down. "You understood what I said?" She asked in Welsh. "I mean, when I was unconscious? Juanita said that you understood."

"Some of it." He smiled and nodded. "I understood the Welsh."

"What was I saying?"

"Oh, nonsense about cats and forests," he waved it off as inconsequential. "You were delirious, I think. But you were speaking another language as well, something I've not heard for a long time. Breton. I don't understand it well enough, certainly not now after all of these decades to know what you were saying."

No secrets had been lost. She could relax. "I was delirious. It was probably nonsense."

"Probably," he agreed. "But it is a curious mix, and Juanita thinks you are Argentinean. How did you come to speak all of these languages?"

"I could ask you the same thing."

He laughed. "Ah-ha. Yes, yes. But these days I don't speak anything from my own land. What I am using today I got from my wives and my adoptive homeland." He spread his arms out. "I live in Argentina, so I speak Spanish. My wife is of Welsh extraction; her parents moved over here before she was born, you know, and brought her up in the Welsh language. So tell me, what is your story, Isobella... I'm sorry," he interrupted himself. "Have we even been introduced? I am Padraig, but you call me Patrick."

"I'm Isobella Omnes."

He raised his eyebrows. "Omnes? My. There is a name I've not heard for so long." His gaze drifted out of the window and they were silent for some time. Silence did not bother Isobella, and she made no attempt to continue the conversation. He broke it with a cough. "Miss Omnes, you have awoken many memories for me. The best and the worst of times, a long time ago. First with your Breton, and then with your name. My first wife was a Breton."

"My mother was Breton. She's dead now, many years ago." Isobella lowered her eyes.

"And so you have the family name Omnes."

"I only took it later on. That was her maiden name. Really my family name is from my father, Donagh. He was Irish."

Patrick stared at her in confusion. "Such coincidence."

"Sorry?"

"Do not worry about it. Life is sometimes strange. Of course we cannot be talking about the same people, for there are generations between you and I. When I was a young man, and this is before the Second World War, you understand, I went out to Brittany and met the love of my life. I'm only telling you this because Gwyneth has passed on. Ahes Omnes she was called. So beautiful, just...." words failed him and he looked away. "She broke my heart. I did not think I would ever mend. But Gwyneth found me, and we have been happy. But Ahes, she did a terrible thing. I have forgiven her. The times were a struggle. She came back to Ireland with me and it cannot have been easy. Then of course there were no children, we were not able, you understand. I think that drove her to chase that man. She followed him over the seas, to Wales. Poor Ahes."

Isobella could feel her stomach knotting up.

"Of course, as you already know, I am a grandfather. Not that I like to phrase it as such, but clearly I had not been the problem. Ahes had been barren. I hope she found peace in the end."

"No, she was not barren. She had me."

He smiled gently at her. "My dear girl, you could not be the daughter of my Ahes, even if she had not been barren. Granddaughter, perhaps, but as I said, none of that would have

138

been possible." He settled back into his chair. "Just a strange coincidence.

She could feel her internal organs contracting up against her spine in terror. "But my mother was Ahes..."

"Just a coincidence. There are certainly many women with that name. Tell me, how is it that you are travelling here in Argentina?"

The floor creaked as Juanita returned with a tray holding a jug of smoky liquid, and clear glasses. Isobella swallowed back her sobs and pressed her shaking fingers into her lap. She watched as the girl poured out two drinks, setting everything on a small side table between them, before retreating back into the depths of the house.

"Why are you here in Argentina?"

"I've been travelling. For a long time," she spoke quietly. "I've been looking for the place where I belong."

"But I can hear it in your voice," he told her. "And you're a long way from home."

She did not know what to think. In some moments she was numb, in others apathetic, or even disbelieving. Then there were the moments when she was furious. Not only had she failed to answer the question of where she belonged, but doubts had been cast over who she was. Maybe it had all been a terrible mistake. The man in Argentina, Patrick Donagh, could have been a coincidence. The Patrick Donagh whom Ahes Omnes had married had died in South America a long time ago. And those people, Ahes and Patrick, since departed, had conceived a child together. Isobella. She had to come from somewhere. She couldn't just be someone's thought who had suddenly appeared overnight, taken in by Ahes and kept secret in the forest for all those formative years.

There had been no paperwork and no record of her. Mr Griffiths, the local solicitor had spent a lot of time and effort in resolving that problem so that she might join contemporary society. No birth certificate. No words on paper to say, yes, you are real and this is where you came from. Nothing.

Isobella, who had been so passive and assuming, had moments when she was full of uncontrollable rage. A switch in her brain flicked and the wrath poured forth. She almost growled at mere existence, her hands slipping forward through the wet, sticky blood as she moved to the end of the bed. Her head was throbbing. It felt as though the room was swaying side to side as though she were on board a ship. She had to claw up handfuls of wet bed sheets to keep her balance. Her vision was flickering, her pupils wavering slightly as if thinking about contracting again. She wanted to scream. She wanted to destroy. There was nothing more to do here.

She stood up from the bed, holding her arms out to steady herself. The ship in her mind righted and the storm calmed. Leaving bloody footprints behind, she walked to the bathroom to take a shower. Behind her rested the last remains of an American pilot who had been idle at the most inopportune moment. He'd had some fun, but had started to wonder towards the end if this woman wasn't getting a little too dominant. A little too much. He'd never seen the knife, but in his last conscious moments he'd assumed there must have been one because there was blood everywhere and he was struggling to breathe.

She could not stop. There was nothing else certain that she knew how to do. Unconsciously she was returning back to the forests of Wales she knew so well, but to do what? There was no purpose for her being here. No home. No family. She was an angel out of hell, raging damnation and murder on a slow path from London towards that cottage in the woods. She took men up on their offers whenever and however. In the darkened alleys, in cheap hotel rooms, in the toilets of pubs, or out in the countryside. They were always stupidly willing, keen to get their hands on the pretty girl and thoughtless to any consequences of their actions. She butchered every damn one of them, sometimes not even waiting until the climax before letting the blow flow. And Isobella was becoming careless. She didn't tidy up the scene on her way. Her homeland had moved on since she had been last there. Words such as a forensics and DNA were commonplace, and professionals in white suits combed the scenes, picking up every trace, be it bagged or photographed, that might explain away what had happened.

Something had to give, and the beginning of the end came to her when she was ambling down a lane, freshly washed after slicing up a one night stand in his holiday cabin. One glance and fate was decided.

She was travelling ever closer to the village, and although she was now in Wales she hadn't quite made it home. She could have been there weeks ago but something held her back. She was desperate to see home and yet scared it had changed too much or would reject her again. So she circled the intended destination, hopping from town to town.

It was dark and nearing ten o'clock at night when she approached the little town. She'd been up at a holiday cabin site just outside of town with a lusty man. Now that the act was committed she needed to be away, back to the inn where she was staying in Machynlleth. The buses did not run that frequently, and although there were cars to be bought and taxis to be phoned for, Isobella still thought of this area as being trapped in the times of her childhood, long before so many options had been available. She was stuck in the past in many respects.

As she walked around the corner, slinking in her heels and red dress, she collided with a man who had been walking out of a pub towards a line of parked cars on the opposite side of the road. There was the dull thud of unexpected bodily collision, then they both stumbled backwards, apologetic at the basic level and not keen to engage with others. They might have each shuffled on in their own separate direction, never really paying attention to each other. He was checking his phone; she was focused on putting one foot in front of another. Only that they both glanced up at the same moment and met one another's gaze. The woman with the deep dark eyes and tousled hair. The man with round eyes and messy hair, so reminiscent of a farm hand she had vaguely known in the village all those years ago that she almost cried out. Sometimes all it takes is a moment.

He smiled lopsidedly. "Sorry about that," he repeated. "I'm not usually this unobservant."

"My fault," she contradicted, moving forward and wobbling on her heels a little. She was coming off the tincture high.

He caught her by the elbow. A spark went through the skin to skin contact. "Bad night?"

"Something like that."

"Me too," he sympathised. "Not a good one. I remembered why I should never agree to blind dates. Fucking hell." He looked up at the night sky. "Your night any better?"

"About the same."

"And you're on your way home now."

"I have to get a bus back to where I'm staying. They don't go too often so I'll have to wait somewhere." She glanced at the pub he had just wandered out of. It looked as good a place as anywhere.

"Look, I don't mean to be forward," he started up as she moved to go in through the door, desperate not to lose her attention. "Do you mind if I join you? I could do with a bit of decent conversation so the night isn't a complete write-off. We could commiserate." He paused, misreading her expression. "I don't even know your name, I know, but it's funny, us bumping into one another like that."

"Isobella Omnes."

He was speechless for a moment. "Omnes," he repeated, shaking sense into his head. "Never heard that before. You're not local?"

"Oh no, I come from a little village relatively close. I've not been back for a while."

"Which village?"

She told him the name.

"Really? No way," he laughed. "My grandparents live there. Funny, I've never seen you about, although you've been away a while, you say? I didn't grow up there, but I'm from round this way..."

She already had worked out that much, she could tell from his dialect.

"Should we...?" he gestured to the pub.

"You've not told me your name yet."

"It's Garreth," he told her, still not quite able to believe his luck. "Garreth Jones."

Of course it was. She nodded as she followed him into the pub.

They settled into a corner table and talked long into the night, far past the time last bus went. Isobella could not quite catch her breath over his uncanny resemblance to that farm worker of long ago. It gave her a giddy internal feeling, an intense yearning she'd not felt before. She answered his questions, spoke at ease on many subjects, although on herself she was suitably open whilst remaining utterly vague so as to commit to nothing of value, yet sound as though she had nothing to hide. She spun a tale of moving back having worked abroad for many years. She was staying at a cheap bed and breakfast before she found somewhere to rent. It sounded plausible. He in turn was the local boy made good. He'd gone to London and lived there for some years, before getting a promotion which meant he could move back to the Welsh office. Isobella didn't notice, but he was just as vague at providing details when it came to the subject of work.

Neither looked for the time until the pub was closing.

"When was your last bus?"

She glanced at the clock. "I've missed it."

"Sorry, that's me, keeping you talking."

"No matter. It's been a better ending to the night than I had expected."

"Agreed. Look, it's my fault you missed your bus. Let me drive you back."

"Oh no, I couldn't..."

"It's on the way."

She paused before agreeing. "All right."

Settling into the passenger seat, Isobella gazed out into the dark Welsh night as he took her on the short journey to Machynlleth. It was with some regret when he pulled up on the high street and she saw they had arrived. She had not wanted to part so quickly. Clicking open the passenger door, she slipped out of the car. "Thank you."

"Wait, Isobella," he pulled against the seat belt, watching her from the car. "Could I get your number? It would be a shame just to disappear into the horizon and..."

"My number?"

"You know, your phone number."

"I told you, I'm not sure where I'm going to be living yet."

"Yes, but what about your mobile number?"

"Mobile? Oh, I never felt the need for one of those."

He broke out into laughter. "You are something special, you know that?"

She couldn't help but grin back.

"All right, I'll have to get in touch with you via the inn. Look, I'll give you my number." He scrabbled in his jacket pocket and pulled out a business card. Turning it over he scribbled his personal number on the back before passing it to her. "I'll maybe see you again."

Isobella smiled. "Maybe."

She stood and watched the car drive away, surprised by how her heart was thumping. Surprised by the fact that she didn't want to take him to her room, stride over him and then slit his throat. This was all very new. A strange chemistry that had finally worked. She was utterly distracted, clutching the card like some precious love token. She gazed at the hand written number. Had she not been quite so smitten she might have flicked the card over and seen what was printed on the front. Realised that she could never see him again.

She had not slept much that night, despite her heavy head and coming off the tincture. Despite the energy slump from murder. All of that was forgotten. When it was morning she virtually floated down the corridor to the breakfast room, thinking to herself that life had never felt so positive.

The landlord stood in the doorway to the dining room, hands on hips as if holding in his sagging belly with little success. He watched the television, a look of distaste worsening as the seconds went by. "It's a bloody disgrace," he grumbled to no one, shaking his head as the news article finished. He moved to step back before sensing there was someone behind him, and glanced around, seeing the pretty European who had turned up a few days ago. It was a bit out of season for tourists, but one could never tell with these foreigners. Her name looked Irish but her accent sounded a bit French or Spanish. He and his wife had discussed it at some length but they had failed to reach any definite conclusion.

She smiled politely. "Has something happened?"

"Some bloody tourist got himself killed."

"An accident?"

"A murder." The Welshman's eyes widened as if to play up the horror. "Sounds like it was a bloody butcher job. Last thing we need round here, scaring off the precious few tourists we get. Of course, you've nothing to worry about," he quickly added. "It was a bloke who was murdered."

"Aye, but whoever did it is bound to be mad, so they'd go for anyone," one of the other guests, already part way through a full breakfast, shouted out to them.

"Ignore him," the landlord advised. "Talking out of his arse. Besides, there's been a lot of this in the news lately, fellas getting slashed up. If you ask me some bloody mad poofter's out at it..."

"Bloody mad poofter?" the guest at breakfast chortled. "Bloody Hell, which century did they dig you up from?"

Isobella smiled awkwardly and slipped into the room. She sat down at a small table set for two, and just took coffee and toast, quietly watching the news. She had never been particularly interested in current events or politics, instead letting the world drift by her. The comings and goings of other people had nothing to do with her. She had never considered that her acts may have garnered much interest beyond the police when they discovered the corpse. Naturally she'd seen the odd newspaper article, searching for information, looking for a witness to an Italian man's death.

As the news programme came to a close they quickly went through the main headlines again, mentioning the gruesome discovery early this morning of a brutalised man in one of the holiday cabins further up the valley. The media must have been tipped off to have already had a cameraman at the crime scene. In the grey morning light it looked rather a drab place. There wasn't much on the article, just an exterior shot of the cabin from a distance, and a lot of guessing on the journalist's part. The man's relatives would not have been informed yet, so the police were not releasing the name. Already bored, she started to lower her eyes to her toast, but flicked back up to the screen when she thought she saw Garreth Jones in the background of the shot. She must have been mistaken. Now that she watched properly, she couldn't see him. It must have been her imagination.

When finished, she got up and walked back into the corridor. The landlord was looming out of the reception hatch, talking to someone. "Isobella Donagh?" He said loudly in the form of a question.

Isobella stopped and looked around at the sound of her name.

"Isobella," he grinned. "There's someone here to see you."

Her face broke out into a smile when she saw it was Garreth. He looked equally pleased. "Hope it's not too early. I was driving past on work and thought I'd stop in on the off chance."

"Not a problem."

He looked smart, still in the suit, and this time with a three quarter length coat. A business man on the way to work. In comparison she probably looked like a scruffy hiker in jeans and a slightly shapeless knitted jumper.

"Things have gotten a bit manic again with work, so I can't stop long," he said. "And I've got to make time for a family dinner this evening. My grandfather's there. We're not sure how much longer he's going to be around, so I've got to make it. Sorry..." he interrupted himself, a little amused by the chatter. "You don't want to know all that. I wanted to ask whether you're free tomorrow evening."

It felt like an age to wait but she wasn't going to turn him down. "Sure."

"Shall I pick you up about half six?"

"Here?"

"Yes."

They loitered in the front hallway, both eager and yet awkward, wanting to lunge in for the kiss but knowing it was too early, and worried it might be misconstrued or taken as too eager. They laughed awkwardly.

"Until tomorrow, then."

She smiled. "Looking forward to it."

The time could not go quickly enough for Isobella, but she would find enough to fill her time until they could meet again. She returned to her room to fetch her coat and put her boots on, then went out walking for the day. She left the town and headed for the surrounding hills, slipping into the forests. These woodlands were not her woodland, but they bore many similarities, and it felt like a prelude to her homecoming to be here. The leaves had just turned, with hues of gold and orange and red fluttering above. Her footsteps rustled through fallen leaves. She found a comfortable little glade deep in the woodland, a perfect curl in an aged trunk against a bank of earth. It was formed just to rock her to sleep. She slipped into the shape, and pulling her collar up around her, fell into a deep sleep.

She woke at some point during dusk, but merely shuffled around and fell asleep again. When she woke properly it was deep night. Isobella sat up as she heard the call of an owl. Brushing leaves off her legs, she stumbled to her feet and stretched. She ought to head back for the inn.

Back in town the pubs were emptying out and people were going home. It had been a good party night, and most were in a jovial mood, feeling over confident from the drink and the banter. Groups of friends and colleagues broke apart as they headed for home in separate directions. One man swaggered out of the centre of town, hands stuffed in his jeans pockets, collar of his leather jacket pulled up as if he were the original cool dude.

Ahead there was a lone woman walking towards him. As they grew closer he felt his breath catch as he saw her beauty. Normally he would never have tried his luck, but with a beer too many in him, anything seemed possible. He called out to her as they were near to passing on opposite sides of the road. She stopped and looked over at him, the movement shifting her hair to tumble in black waves down the side of her face.

He didn't recognise her, certainly wasn't a local. Might be a tourist, maybe didn't even speak Welsh, but he tried another line. He couldn't quite believe it when she replied in the mother tongue. She had turned to face him directly, her hips at an inviting angle. Not even bothering to check for oncoming traffic, he went out across the road. She smiled as he stepped up to her, close enough to feel the heat of her body.

"*Noz vat,*" she whispered.

Isobella was ready a half hour in advance, with special attention paid to her appearance. She'd slept off her tincture hangover and woken fresh in the afternoon. With hair washed, dried and brushed, make up applied, she looked youthful and expectant. Ready for a new chapter. She loitered in the front hall of the inn, ignoring the knowing smiles of the landlord who had overheard yesterday and knew exactly what was going on. A story played over on infinite occasions.

Garreth was late, and it was nearing seven when he arrived. He seemed distracted, almost melancholy, and would only begrudgingly meet her eye as he entered the inn. Isobella bounced up to her feet, needing all her control not to fling her arms about him.

"Shall we head off then?" he asked. "I don't want to stay here. Let's go to one of the villages."

"Sure." She didn't care where it was as long as they were together.

He turned the radio on in the car to cover over the silence. He drove through the darkness as if he were alone. Isobella watched him warily. "Was it a busy day at work?" Hopefully he was just tired and hadn't changed his mind about her.

"Yes," he sighed. "I got called in to work just after six. I've only just gotten away." He paused, looking grim as he turned off at a junction. "Not that it goes away."

They pulled up at a pub in a little village, ordering drinks and food at the bar, then finding a secluded table by a darkened window. There was an open fire crackling across the room, and the faint smell of firewood. Garreth remained distant, staring out of the window to nothing. Either that or vaguely watching her

150

reflection. Isobella slowly turned her drink around on one of the cardboard beer mats. She hoped he had not cooled this quickly for her.

"Is your work very demanding?"

He looked at her questioningly as if she were mad. "You know what I do."

"You've not really talked that much..."

"I gave you my card."

"Yes, but that was just your mobile. I..." she drifted off. She'd had that card in her jacket pocket, fingering it like a love token but she'd never looked at it that much. She took it out now, flipping it over from the hand written personal mobile number. It made sense. A horrible truth. She looked up at him. "You're a detective. You work for the police."

He looked surprised that this was news to her. "It goes in peaks and troughs, and we've going through a bad phase at the moment. There's been a spate of nasty murders. When you mark them on a map it looks like a drunken route drawn out from London to Wales. I was in the graveyard at St Peter's this morning, in Machynlleth."

"That's why you didn't want to eat in town."

"You must have heard about it; it's just down the road from where you're staying."

Isobella looked down at her drink. She'd been asleep all day.

"Local lad got his throat slashed. Looks like he'd gone into the graveyard for a quick shag. God knows why because he only lived a five minute walk away. Not a dignified way to go, with your pants round your knees. Fucking blood everywhere. Then yesterday I was up at a holiday cabin, just outside that village where we first met. A tourist was killed, just the same, with his throat slit. The arterial spray was all over the bedroom walls, the sheets. He'd just had sex as well. We've taken all kinds of samples. Thing is, we're hoping for a match. There's been traces of vaginal secretions at previous murder sites, and they've matched. There's a psychopathic woman wandering around murdering these tossers. And we've got to figure all this out and stop it repeating."

She felt a cold sweat pricking at the back of her neck. She kept her hands in place on the table where they rested. She didn't want to lift them and betray a shake. Her voice was steady. "There must be a lot you don't understand."

"What I don't understand is you."

Isobella looked up sharply.

Garreth looked as though his heart were breaking. "I went to that family dinner last night, and I was asking my grandfather about the village. I thought he might know your people. He'd never heard of Omnes. But when I was at the inn yesterday the landlord called you Donagh, didn't he? And my grandfather knew about the Donaghs, especially Isobella Donagh. Jesus Christ, he looked like he'd seen a ghost. I thought I'd given him a heart attack.

He told me about Ahes Donagh, a mad woman who lived like a hermit in the forests and sporadically came into the village for supplies. Hit by a delivery truck, killed outright. It only came to light afterwards that she'd had a daughter, Isobella, who'd grown up in isolation in the forests. They brought her to live in the village before she was sent off to London. Absolute stunner by all accounts, I think my grandfather was quite smitten at the time. Some people said she was a witch..."

"That's just..."

"Thing is," Garreth interrupted sharply. "Isobella was the last Donagh to live in the village. What I don't understand who the hell you're supposed to be."

This comment threw her. She'd felt her heart beating up through her throat in convulsions, terrified he was going to accuse her of being a murderess. Of leading him on. Of simply seeing him as nothing more than a victim in a line. She'd never for a moment thought he might question the truth of who she was.

"I had a look in the village graveyard. Ahes Donagh was Ahes Omnes before she married."

"I sometimes go by my mother's maiden name."

"No you don't." He leaned forward. "If Isobella Donagh was even still alive today, she'd be in her eighties. It can be hard to pinpoint people's ages by appearance alone, but you're a young woman and there's no way in hell you're a pensioner."

She looked fearfully to her reflection in the dark window. A young woman stared back at her, terrified by the near future. Glossy black hair without a strand of grey. No wrinkles, no liver spots. Tight, fresh skin. He was right. This was a young woman before him. But she had lived through decades. Who was she?

"Who the hell are you?" He repeated her silent question. "Did you read a death notice and decide to pick up the identity?"

"No."

"That road you were walking down when we first met; you know it goes up to those holiday cabins where that tourist was murdered. He was killed around about the time you and I met, or slightly earlier. That lad I had to go see to this morning was killed just around the corner from where you're staying." He ran a hand over his face. "Maybe I'm just tired and over thinking things. It's only circumstantial, and just because you're pretending to be someone you're not, doesn't mean it's anything more than that. But we have DNA. All we need is a swab that matches."

Isobella could feel something in her chest breaking.

He stood up. "I'm going for a piss. When I get back you need to tell me the truth."

As he walked past they shared a look. They both understood that this wasn't carelessness on his part. The moment he was out of sight Isobella got up and walked out of the building. She left the car park and the street, and slipped into the darkness, moving off down the road out of the village. She climbed over a field gate and dropped into the damp, chilled grass. Somewhere over the far side the sheep flocked together. This was close enough to the village and the forests beyond that she knew the lie of the land. She could find her way home from here in the dark, and she would have to. She broke out into a jog. This was her one final chance.

She kept to the fields and stayed away from the roads. Occasionally her bearings were thrown off kilter when she came upon a house that had not been there when she had last been in the locality. The place where she had grown up had jumped across to the twenty-first century. There were broad, gleaming cars parked by houses, central heating and electric lighting. Satellite dishes attached to the walls to pick up signals from space. At one point, crouched at a hedgerow, she watched a police car rush down a country lane. She wondered if it was out on routine business, or if he'd already felt duty bound to call her in. She couldn't risk being seen by anyone.

It took hours to get back. Cross country walking and clambering slowed her down, as did the necessary avoidance of roads and settlements. She eventually got to the village in the hour before dawn. From a distance she gazed at the sleeping hamlet. It had grown since she had last been there. A seventies housing estate had been attached to the side like an afterthought. She wondered if Miss Rees' cottage was still there and who might be living in it.

Delving into the forest's outer reaches, she felt a touch of relief for the first time. Almost there. The woodland landscape had changed. The trees had grown older and thicker, and some had been removed, either by disease or thinning by man. Certain blocks had been completely harvested and new batches of trees planted, mere saplings to what she remembered. She was exhausted, but the visible changes sent a panic through her and she started to run. She needed to be home, to assure herself that it was still there. Not all was lost.

The cottage was still secluded deep within what remained of the forest. Forgotten and unknown, it had not been inhabited by humans since Isobella had last been here. It now stood in ruins. The roof had collapsed in a long time ago, and subsequent wind and rain had destroyed the fabrics and papers stored inside, rotting everything away to dank hunks of grime. The front door had decayed on its hinges and gradually collapsed, soft splinters scattering on the overgrown garden path. The entrance was now just a gaping hole, poorly lighted as dawn rose upon the land. Isobella touched the stone wall as she stepped in through the shabby doorway. Beyond the kitchen area the cottage had utterly fallen in on itself and was just a tumble of stone. Plants grew through the refuse pile, reaching for sunlight. Bird droppings covered everything. Glass in the surviving windows was broken and a spider's web dangled in the hole. A growing sapling pushed up against the side of the building, and eventually it would win, tearing down the wall.

Isobella held the sob in the back of her throat. Time and neglect had taken its toll on the house. Time had taken everything, as was the natural course. Ahes was long dead, the cottage was in ruins. Ahes' estranged husband, if he were still alive now, was back in Argentina, a withered husk of what he once was. Everything moved with the passage of time. Everything but Isobella.

She held out her smooth hands in front of her. "What's wrong with me?"

She would not see Garreth again. She could never hope for decades with him, happily aging together. She was utterly incapable. She cried out and fled from the cottage. The garden was overgrown, a mixture of plants uncontrolled and new saplings as the forest reclaimed the land. She pushed through the waist-high plants and batted away the spreading branches of trees.

In the corner by the wall and the cottage, she dropped to her knees at the old bed of *atropa belladonna*. Deadly nightshade. It still flourished here. Source of the tincture. This plant had sustained Ahes, and at times it had been all that Isobella had lived for. She started to cry, scrabbling in the earth like a wild animal, digging into the dirt, wrenching up roots and stalks. Mud got stuck under her fingernails, rocks and plant matter tore at her flesh and her hands become bloodied. She was numb to the pain and continued to dig by hand. Leaves got caught up in her hair. Earth piled up around her legs, making her a part of the garden, half planted.

Her fingers hit something hard, and she stopped, pushing bruised fingertips down. She dug more of the earth away before grabbing a hold on the object and pulling it out. She held a leg bone aloft, dirty and desiccated, long since it had carried flesh. She stared at it. A human leg bone. There used to be a witch living at the cottage, they would say. When was that? Was it before her time? She dropped the leg bone and started to dig. Sweat poured down, cutting channels through the dirt on her face and her arms.

In another hour or so, she had excavated most of the body. There were ribs and finger bones, arms, hips and shoulder blades scattered around her. The skull lay in place in the dank hole. Broken stems of belladonna lay in the shadows like goodbye flowers from a funeral. The plant still rushed up around the edges, taking sleight at the disturbance. Sitting back on her haunches and breathing heavily, Isobella gazed around what she had dug up. Who was this? Who was she?

Her arms shook in exhaustion. Isobella closed her eyes and slumped down, rolling into the hole and catching a few of the bones on her way, pulling them down with her. She lay on her back, utterly spent. The breeze moved through the belladonna still standing. The deep earth chill crept over the sweat, turning it to ice before seeping through her flesh. She opened her eyes and stared up at the forest canopy. She would sleep and tonight ice crystals would form in her hair. Her lips would turn blue. She would gently become part of the forest again.

She plucked a handful of berries from the plant and took them raw, swallowing them. Turning to her side, she lay in a foetus position and closed her eyes. It was time to dream.